the
trouble
with
half a
moon

To Hafsa —
Remember to believe
even when you
cannot See.

:)

3 eyes r better
than 1 !

the trouble with half a moon

DANETTE VIGILANTE

G. P. Putnam's Sons
An Imprint of Penguin Group (USA) Inc.

G. P. PUTNAM'S SONS
A division of Penguin Young Readers Group.
Published by The Penguin Group. Penguin Group (USA) Inc., 375 Hudson Street, New York, NY
10014, U.S.A. Penguin Group (Canada), 90 Eglinton Avenue East, Suite 700, Toronto, Ontario
M4P 2Y3, Canada (a division of Pearson Penguin Canada Inc.). Penguin Books Ltd, 80 Strand, London
WC2R 0RL, England. Penguin Ireland, 25 St. Stephen's Green, Dublin 2, Ireland (a division of Penguin
Books Ltd.). Penguin Group (Australia), 250 Camberwell Road, Camberwell, Victoria 3124, Australia
(a division of Pearson Australia Group Pty Ltd). Penguin Books India Pvt Ltd, 11 Community Centre,
Panchsheel Park, New Delhi—110 017, India. Penguin Group (NZ), 67 Apollo Drive, Rosedale, North
Shore 0632, New Zealand (a division of Pearson New Zealand Ltd). Penguin Books (South Africa) (Pty)
Ltd, 24 Sturdee Avenue, Rosebank, Johannesburg 2196, South Africa. Penguin Books Ltd, Registered
Offices: 80 Strand, London WC2R 0RL, England.

Printed in the United States of America.
Design by Richard Amari.
Text set in Garamond.

Library of Congress Cataloging-in-Publication Data
Vigilante, Danette. The trouble with half a moon / Danette Vigilante. p. cm. Summary: Overwhelmed
by grief and guilt over her brother's death and its impact on her mother, and at odds with her best friend,
thirteen-year-old Dellie reaches out to a neglected boy in her building in the projects and learns from a
new neighbor to have faith in herself and others. [1. Grief—Fiction. 2. Faith—Fiction. 3. Child abuse—
Fiction. 4. Friendship—Fiction. 5. Public housing—Fiction. 6. City and town life—Fiction. 7. Puerto
Ricans—Fiction. 8. Jamaican Americans—Fiction.] I. Title. PZ7.V6688Tro 2011 [Fic]—dc22
2010007377
ISBN 978-0-399-25159-7
5 7 9 10 8 6 4

For my parents, George and Louise.
Especially to my gram, Chi-Chi.
You are always in my heart.

the trouble with half a moon

ONE

The noise wakes up the entire building. It's louder than loud, like a firecracker.

Before I know what I'm doing, I'm out of bed. My parents are already in the dark living room.

None of our neighbors dare go out into the hallway. Instead, they stay behind their doors asking questions through the cracks.

"What's going on out there?" Mr. Brown, from apartment 2C, asks. His voice sounds croaky with sleep.

"Everything okay?" That sounds like Mrs. Lawrence. She's really old and lives by herself in 2F. I imagine her hunched over by the door with her hand on the doorknob, listening for an answer.

A woman is screaming and there's some loud crying. It starts and stops like a car trying to jump to life. My best friend, Kayla, lives upstairs near the roof door, so I hope whatever is happening isn't coming from there.

When my father grabs his baseball bat, I know he's also worried. "It's June, too early for firecrackers," he says. "That was a gunshot."

"Oh, no," my mother says. There have been shootings in other buildings around here, but this is the first time it's happened where I live.

My teeth start to chatter. I can't make them stop, not even when I clench them. "Daddy, please move away from the door. They might shoot again." It comes out funny and I have to say it a second time. But instead of moving, he looks through the peephole. Every apartment in the projects has one. My mother tells me never to open the door without looking through it first.

"*Tenga cuidado,*" my mother says.

"Don't worry. I'll be careful." Dad presses his ear against our door. "Maybe someone needs help. I'll go see if there's anything I can do."

"But I don't hear any noise now. Do you?" I whisper, watching for his thick eyebrows to answer me first. "Do you? Maybe whatever it was is over now. It could be, right? Let's just go back to bed." He doesn't move. "Please!"

My mother shushes me and leads me to the couch.

I bring my knees to my chin and stretch my nightgown over my legs. My mother sits next to me and holds my hand.

"I have to go see if everything is okay, Dellie," my father says, unlocking the door.

"No, you might get hurt! You don't know who's out there."

"She's right, it's not a good idea," my mother says, tightening her grasp on my hand. "I need you to stay where I know you're safe."

"I'll be okay," he says, opening the door and letting the hallway light flood the room. The veins in his hands bulge as he grips the bat.

"Dad, no! That can't stop a bullet." Panic pushes its way into my head and causes a quiet terror inside me. The air has been sucked out of the room and I can't catch my breath no matter how hard I try. My eyes go blurry and I can't see. I don't want to do this again. Please, make it stop.

"I'll be fine. Lock the door after I leave. I won't be long," my father says, stepping into the hallway.

The room feels darker now that my father is on the other side of the door.

After my mother locks up, she turns a lamp on and then dusts my brother Louis's picture. My great-grandmother's rosary beads are draped over the frame. They're from Puerto Rico and are very old. The last time we visited my relatives in Puerto Rico, my aunt Evie tried to give us another set, but my mother refused. She said new ones don't hold as much power as old ones do.

Angel figurines and a white candle surround my brother's

smiling face. Mom dusts the picture twice a day and each time I wonder if my parents think I'm to blame.

We sit together on the couch and hold hands for a long time. Even though they're getting sweaty, I won't let go. Not until my father comes back.

"Where is he?" my mother whispers.

Somewhere, a door slams and we jump. My heart is racing. Another door, then loud talking fills the hallway.

My father's voice is nowhere in any of the noise.

"It doesn't take this long to see if somebody needs help, Mom," I say, looking at my brother's picture. "You know right away."

As soon as the police sirens go from low and faraway to loud and close, the panic lets go of me. They're almost here, which means my father won't have to help anymore.

When the police cars are right outside our building, blue and red streaks dance all over our living room, even across my mother's worried face.

After a few minutes, there's a knock on the door. I know it's my father because he always knocks the same way. Seven taps in a row, like a song just starting, but my mother still looks through the peephole to be sure.

"Are you okay?" my mother says, squeezing my father tight.

"Yes, I'm fine."

"What happened?" I ask.

"Someone fired a gun into one of the doors on the first floor, but, thank God, no one was hurt. We can all go back to sleep now."

There's no way I'll be able to sleep, thinking about the bullet and what could've happened if it was our door.

After Mom and Dad tuck me in, their hushed voices go on until the birds start chirping. I guess I'm not the only one who can't sleep.

TWO

I'm lying on my bed listening to music after school when somebody knocks lightly on our door. At first I think it's Kayla, but she never knocks so softly. I turn the radio off and hear it again. I don't see anything through the peephole but then there's another knock, and a small voice.

"Do you have a piece of bread for me?" I think it's Corey. I've heard him asking other people in our building for food a couple of times. He and his mother moved in on the first floor last month. It was their apartment door that last night's bullet got buried in.

My father's bat is still sitting in the corner.

When I open the door, the bat falls and bounces against the floor. Corey covers his head and crouches down.

"It's just my father's baseball bat," I say.

Corey straightens up and I see his clothes haven't been washed in a while. His white shirt has brown stains on it and his pants have dry mud on the hems.

Corey lets a smile escape. "I'm not a chicken. That's silly."

His teeth are like pieces of white chewing gum, the way my brother's teeth used to look. His skin is the color of caramel.

"Where's your mother?" I ask him.

He looks down at the floor and shrugs his bony shoulders.

"Why are you always hungry?"

When Corey looks up, I see that tears are sitting in his eyes waiting to drop. "Because there's nothing to eat in my house," he answers. Then he looks at Mr. Brown's door. "Mr. Brown gives me stuff to eat, but he didn't answer his door today."

Corey needs more than just a piece of bread. He's much skinnier than Louis was. Louis loved to eat.

"How about a peanut butter and jelly sandwich?"

Corey rubs his belly with both hands. "Yes!"

I'm not allowed to have any company when my parents aren't home, but I don't think they'll mind since the company is just a hungry little boy.

"Man, you're rich, right?" Corey asks, looking around at our things.

"No," I say, trying to see our apartment the way Corey is seeing it. It's clean and we have what we need, but nothing else.

Corey watches me make us sandwiches. I make his thicker than mine and pour two glasses of milk.

"I don't like milk," he says.

"How about if I make yours chocolate milk?"

He pokes a finger out from each hand and pumps them into the air. "Yes!" He laughs.

Corey wiggles into a kitchen chair and eats his sandwich right away. While he chews, he hums just like Louis used to and that sets panic into motion. My chest feels tight and my breath comes too quick. With shaky hands, I pull out a seat.

"Hey," Corey nudges my arm. "What's the matter with you?"

"Nothing," I say after a minute.

"Are you sure? 'Cause I'm five years old and I've got big muscles. See?" He flexes his arms and puffs out his little chest. "I can help."

"Thanks, but I'm fine now." I smile.

"Okay. So, how old are you?" Corey asks.

"I'm thirteen."

"And what's your name?"

"Delilah, but everybody just calls me Dellie."

"Who? Everybody like your friends?"

"Yup."

He sits forward. "Can *I* call you Dellie and be your friend too?" he asks, watching me closely.

I almost say no, but he's got jelly on his chin and he's swinging his legs and I think he's cute. "Okay."

"Yes!" he says.

"You sure like to say yes a lot, huh?"

Corey looks to the ceiling and giggles. "Yes."

After a few seconds, his name rings through the hallway. "Corey! Corey!" his mother calls. He quiets down right away, like he's been caught doing something bad. His fun turns off like it has a switch. "I gotta go now, Dellie."

He hops off the chair and wipes his mouth on his sleeve. "I'll come up and see you again, okay?"

"Okay," I say, opening the door for him.

He runs down the stairs, calling, "Here I am, Mommy," over and over.

THREE

Every day, me and Kayla walk to and from school together. It's only a short walk, but my mother makes my father come with us. He knows I'm too big to be brought to school, so he follows behind me at a distance in the morning so he won't embarrass me. He used to take an afternoon break from work to walk me home but stopped when he saw I was all right on my own. He said there was no reason to worry my mother, so we've never told her.

Today, Kayla knocks just as my parents are getting ready for work. She's wearing thick box braids pulled back into a bun. The skirt she's wearing shows off her long legs.

"Come in, Kayla," my father says. "Do you want some breakfast?"

"No, thanks, I've eaten already."

"Hey Kayla," my mother says, giving Louis's picture one last swipe with a dust rag. "I'd better get going." She kisses me before walking out the door.

On the way to school I sneak a peek over my shoulder to make sure my father is far enough away to not hear me. "That kid Corey from the first floor came up to my house looking for food yesterday."

"Did you give him any?" Kayla asks.

"Of course. How could I not? He's adorable."

"Yeah, he is. What did your parents say?"

"They don't know," I answer, thinking about how much he reminded me of Louis.

"Are you going to tell them?"

"I don't think that's a good idea."

Kayla nods, knowing what I mean. "You're right."

When we get to the corner of school, I give my father the usual sneaky good-bye wave so nobody will see, and continue through the gates.

In homeroom, Shayna's filing her nails. She's got a whole manicure kit spread out on her desk. "Anybody want me to hook their nails up for them? Only three bucks. What about you, Dellie?" she says, grabbing my hand as I pass. She makes a face. "Oh, no, for you . . . ten dollars. Your fingernails are seriously messed up."

I pull my hand away.

"Very funny," Kayla says. "Nobody wants you touching them with your skanky file anyway."

When our homeroom teacher, Mr. Lang, walks in, Shayna focuses her attention on him. "Do you want me to go to the office and get your mail or something, Mr. L.?" Shayna's such a kiss up.

"That won't be necessary. And please, put that stuff away." He points to her kit.

After Mr. Lang takes attendance, the bell rings.

I walk into the crowded hallway while Kayla gathers up her books. A bunch of boys are hanging around the water fountain. One of them is Michael Ortiz, a boy from my math class. He's cute and smart. His wavy hair is dark and thick and he wears it kind of long, down to his shoulders. Sometimes, when he lifts his head after the teacher has called on him, his hair falls in front of his face and blocks one eye. He never bothers to move it.

When I get closer, I hear "There she is." I look around to see who they're talking about, but it's too busy to see who they mean.

I tell Kayla about it later at lunch. "They must've been talking about you."

"Yeah, right." I tear open a pack of chips.

"I'm serious."

"What would make you think something ridiculous like that?" I ask.

"Remember two weeks ago," Kayla says, stealing a chip, "when you dropped your juice . . ."

"I don't think anybody will ever forget that day. It took all afternoon for my pants to dry. People called me Pee-Pee Pants for a week."

"You're leaving out the most important part," Kayla finishes.

"You don't think being Miss Pee-Pee Pants for a week is important?"

"Jeez! Are you going to let me finish?"

I nod and pop a chip into my mouth.

"The important part is that Michael went to get you another juice. He didn't even ask you for the money. Come to think of it," Kayla says, "you're the one he comes to when he needs a pen even though other people sit closer to him. I'm telling you, he likes you."

I think about Michael and how, when he smiles, his whole face lights up. I swallow my chip. "I never thought about it like that before."

"Well, start thinking," Kayla says, tapping my head.

That's exactly what I do for the rest of the day.

FOUR

Since I first fed Corey last week, he's come up to our second-floor apartment for food a few times while my parents were at work. When they're home, I pack him a banana if we have it, string cheese, some cereal in a baggie and a juice box. Then, I sneak everything to him when I can. I don't want my parents to see him, ever. I worry he'll remind them of Louis just like he reminds me.

A couple of months after the accident, my father finally convinced my mother to go to grief counseling with him, which is where they are this morning. I went too, but the therapist said I was doing okay, so my father decided I didn't have to go anymore.

I guess I'm more of an actress than I thought or the therapist wasn't too smart. If she was, she would've figured out that I sometimes break into a panic so thick it's hard to breathe. Like there's water almost up to my nose and I'm close to drowning. She would've asked me about the bad dreams I have or at least known the accident was all my fault.

Corey knocks on my door and when I open it, he flashes those baby chewing-gum teeth. It makes me feel mixed up inside and I wonder if it was a good idea to tell him we're friends.

"Hi, Dellie. Can I come in today?"

On days like today, having him in my apartment wouldn't work because sometimes, on Saturdays, I can't get myself past the sadness I feel. Louis and I loved to watch morning cartoons together.

"No, not today. My parents are home," I lie.

"Oh," he says quietly.

"Wait here. I'll get some stuff for you to take."

In the kitchen, I fill a bag with the usual things, only we're out of bananas again, so I give him an apple instead.

When I come back, Corey is with Kayla, looking out the hallway window. The window is open and even though he can barely reach it, I tell him to be careful the same way my mother tells me whenever I leave the house.

"Don't worry, I'm watching him," Kayla says. "We were just taking bets on what kind of fruit you were going to give him today."

"Yeah," he says, hurrying over. "If I win, she's going to buy me some gum!"

"Check it out then." I hand the bag to him.

Corey doesn't look at me when he reaches for it. "What's wrong?" I ask.

"You sure I can't come in today, Dellie?"

"I'm sure."

"Please?"

I look to Kayla for help.

"Maybe tomorrow, okay, Corey?" she says. "Let's go sit in the courtyard and see if I need to buy you that gum."

"Okay," he says, making his way down the steps.

It's not right to lie to him but sometimes what's right and what's wrong get jumbled up and you don't know which is which.

I watch from my window as Corey and Kayla sit on a bench in the courtyard. Corey pulls the string cheese out of the bag. Instead of biting it, he flies the wobbly cheese into the air like an airplane. Then he takes the apple out. "I win, Dellie!" he says, waving happily.

"Awww, man," Kayla says playfully. "What kind of gum do you want?"

I hope I'll feel better tomorrow.

Back inside my apartment, I hold my brother's picture and say a prayer, only I'm not sure if it's really a prayer. It's more like I'm just talking to him in my head. I tell him how sorry I am and how much I miss him.

I stay in my room for the rest of the day and even though

I'm allowed to stay up later because it's Saturday, I don't. I fall asleep to the sounds of our courtyard. Summer is coming, but that doesn't mean much to me. My days are spent inside where it's safe. My mother wants me safe.

Sundays are the quietest days in my house. My father lies on the couch watching old black-and-white movies with the volume so quiet, I don't know how he knows what's going on.

Instead of sleeping in, my mother is always up early and cooking even before she finishes her *café con leche*. By the time I get out of bed, the house is filled with the delicious smells of our Sunday dinner: *pernil*, which is roast pork that has to be marinated overnight, *maduros*, sweet plantains, *arroz con gandules*, rice and pigeon peas, a salad with sliced avocado and rolls and butter. In Puerto Rico, people eat like this all the time, not just on Sundays.

For dessert, we used to have chocolate pudding since it was Louis's favorite. But we have ice cream now.

I do my homework at the kitchen table until it's time to eat, then set the table. It took me a long time to get used to setting three places instead of four. In the beginning, when we started to be a family again, I'd forget but my father would remember and take the extra plate and cutlery away before my mother noticed.

"You've outdone yourself today," my father says after his first bite.

My mother smiles weakly and glances at my brother's chair.

"Yeah, Mom," I say, wanting her to think about something else. "Everything is delicious. How old were you when you learned how to cook?" I wonder if she'll teach me soon. I'll be fourteen in six months and it's time for me to learn.

"She was born knowing," my father says dramatically, rubbing his rounded stomach. "And I think she's trying to make me fat. My pants are getting tighter by the day." I guess he noticed my mother's eyes on Louis's chair too.

"I was fourteen," my mother says to me. Then she turns to my father. "You were too skinny when I met you anyway. All bones and no meat!"

She laughs and even though her laugh is missing something, it makes me happy. I'm ready for change. It'll never go back to the way things were but maybe, just maybe, we can find a new way to be.

Kayla comes over after dessert. "Can Dellie come outside with me for a little while?" she asks when my mother answers the door.

"No, honey, not today."

She says it like she'll let me out tomorrow, but I know she won't.

"Why don't you come in?" my mother says.

"I had to try," Kayla says, plopping her books down on my desk. "One day she'll change her mind and say yes."

"Change is never going to happen around here," I say, discouraged again.

Kayla adjusts her headband. "Never say never, Dellie. I bet by the time school is out, you'll be free."

"I think your headband is too tight." I laugh.

We're quiet for a while, then Kayla says, "I'm serious. I'm tired of seeing you at your window when I'm out having fun. Best friends are supposed to have fun together."

"I'm tired of it too." I sigh, taking out my schoolbooks. "We might as well study for the math test." We have a test every Monday and I usually fail or just squeak by.

"When will I ever need this stuff?" I moan, going through some of the problems.

"You need to stop whining and girl-up," Kayla says, air-boxing. "If I can do math, so can you."

Her attitude reminds me of when I first met her. When I returned to school three weeks after the accident, no one said a word to me in the crowded hallways, but I could hear the whispering.

The teachers had pity in their eyes when they looked at me. Some squeezed my shoulder like that would make things better.

When I got to my first class of the day, Kayla was standing outside the door like she'd been waiting for me. She was the new kid in school, but you couldn't tell that by looking at her. She stared everybody in the face like she owned the hallway.

"Hey Dellie, you all right?" she asked. "I'm sorry about what happened. Is there anything I can do to help?"

I watched Kayla silently for a long time. There was nothing anybody could do.

Sophia, our class's loudmouthed troublemaker, came by just then. "Kayla, why are you bothering Dellie?" She poked a finger in Kayla's face. "Don't you know her brother was killed the other day?"

Just when I thought every last tear had dried up, more came down.

"Look what you did," Sophia said. "You made her cry with your stupid self." She turned to me. "She say something mean to you, Dellie? 'Cause I know she ain't got no sense, talking about your dead brother and trying to look all pretty with her cheap weave."

"For your information, my hair is real and you're the one saying stupid things and making her cry." Kayla moved closer to Sophia. "So why don't you just keep on walking with your nasty self?"

Next to Kayla's long, skinny body, Sophia looked extra short.

"Yeah, whatever," Sophia said, walking away. "You're lucky I have to get to class now or I would . . ."

"Uh-huh, that's what I thought," Kayla said.

Sophia never spoke to us again.

. . .

"Girl-up?" I say. "I can't do math like you, Kayla. God gave you a math brain. The only thing I got was . . . I don't know, a plain brain?"

After studying for two hours straight, I've had enough, and stretch out on my bed. My head hurts from trying to squeeze numbers into it.

"Yeah, I could use a break too," Kayla says.

"A break?" I say. "I am so done with this math, it's not even funny."

I get up and go over to the window. Kayla follows.

"Look, there's Corey," she says. He's following another little boy, who's eating a cookie. Corey holds his hand out and the boy puts a tiny piece into it.

"He's hungry all the time and it's not right," I say.

"I know, but what can we do?"

"Try to save him I guess."

"Yeah, how?"

"I have no idea . . ." I couldn't even save my own brother. How could I save anyone else.

When it's time for bed, I toss and turn, worrying that Corey might not have had enough to eat today. That's probably what makes me have another bad dream about Louis.

We're at the beach. The water is blue just like the water in Puerto Rico, only here it's rough and cold. I refuse to go in, but Louis is splashing around like he's in the bathtub. He's holding his favorite stuffed dog, Connie Boy, over his head so it doesn't get wet. "Come in, Dellie," he yells from ankle-deep water. "It's not cold!"

A breeze blows my hair back and gives me goose bumps. I wiggle my toes into the damp sand. "It's cold."

"Fine," he says stubbornly. "I'll have fun by myself and"— he walks farther into the water just as the breeze turns into a strong wind. Bits of sand sting my face and fly into my mouth. When I bite down, they crunch against my teeth— "you won't," he finishes, looking toward me.

Out of nowhere, a wave the size of a building curls over Louis as I watch. He doesn't know it's gathering speed and growing behind him, but I do, and I can't open my mouth in time to warn him. All I can do is feel the panic as it overcomes me.

The crashing of the wave is louder than anything I've ever heard and it's my fault.

I'm up and dressed for school before my alarm goes off.

FIVE

W hat's with the dark circles underneath your eyes?" Kayla asks when she picks me up for school.

Talking about the dream won't do any good, so I don't mention it. "Thanks, you look nice too," I say even though the truth is, she always looks nice. It's hard not to when you've got pretty, light brown eyes and a pimple-free face like she does.

"You girls start walking," my father says. "I just have to grab my wallet from the bedroom. I'll catch up."

"Okay, Dad."

"You know I didn't mean anything by what I said," Kayla says as we leave my apartment.

"Yeah, I know," I answer. "I just had a hard time falling asleep because I couldn't stop worrying about Corey."

"He must be okay or we would've heard something," Kayla says.

I nod. She's probably right.

We wave to Alexa Rodriguez. She lives in the building across from us. She's in our class but has to take her little sister to the babysitter every morning because her mother is already at work. At least twice a week, she's late to school because her sister gives her a hard time. Today, her sister's trying to wiggle away from Alexa and when she can't, she throws herself to the ground. By the looks of it, Alexa is going to be late.

"Come on, brat!" she says, tugging her sister's hand. "I hate taking you to school."

"Chill, Alexa," I say. "You shouldn't pull on her so hard."

"Don't worry about what I'm doing," Alexa says. "Now let's go before I drag you," she growls to her sister.

Her little sister must know she means business because she slowly starts to walk.

"So," Kayla says, "you think you're ready for the test?"

"Me, ready for math?" That's a joke. "Even if I do pass, we've only got a few weeks before school's over. It won't be enough to pass the class."

"You know, Michael is really good in math. Much better than I am," Kayla says. "Maybe you should ask him to tutor you or something."

"What? No way. It'd be embarrassing He's too cute."

"Duh, he's cute. *And*, he likes you," Kayla says, covering

her mouth. "Oops, I'm sorry. You think your dad heard me?"

I take a look behind me and see that he's too far back to hear. "I don't think so."

"Good. Now," she says, looking all shy, "if it was me and there was a chance Bryan could do the tutoring, I'd definitely ask."

"Whoa, you mean left-back-twice Bryan? He's got such a bad attitude. Since when do you like him?"

"I like tall guys and he's been checking me out lately."

"Serious? How come you never told me?"

"I just did." She laughs.

A city bus stops as we get to the corner of school. Bryan steps off and heads right for us. "Speak of the devil . . . ."

"Do I look okay?" Kayla whispers.

"Yeah, relax yourself."

"What's up?" he says to Kayla, completely ignoring me.

"Nothing." She smiles like she's lost her sense.

"Can I talk to you for a minute?" Bryan asks, adjusting his baseball cap.

Kayla nods.

"Um, I was thinking *alone*," he says suddenly. "Without your assistant."

"Kayla, I'll see you in class." I turn to give my father a small wave, then tell Mr. Left Back what my name is before heading into the school building.

∎ ∎ ∎

Just after the bell rings Kayla rushes into homeroom. There's no time to talk and the hallway is way too noisy so I'll have to wait to find out what Bryan wanted.

A man I've never seen before is sitting in Mrs. Robertson's chair when we get to math. He's got a big, fat mustache and puffy hair parted in the middle. His cheeks are red and rough-looking. There's a newspaper spread out on the desk and a cup of coffee next to it. Big letters on the blackboard say *Business as usual. Take your assigned seats.* I guess he doesn't play.

"All right, a sub!" Kayla says. "He probably won't give us the test today. Now you'll have an extra day to study."

"What did Bryan want?" I ask.

"He wanted to know if I had a boyfriend."

"Did you tell him you're not allowed to have one yet?"

"No way," she answers with a smile.

The room is very loud since everybody is talking at the same time. Mrs. Robertson is hardly ever absent and when she is, it's like we're on a minivacation.

Either the sub is deaf or he's got earplugs in because he's not paying any attention to the noise. Not even when Shayna's chair falls over with her in it. Everybody's quiet for a second, then cracks up. It's a good thing she's wearing jeans today and not one of her short skirts.

We take our seats. I sit in one of the middle rows. Kayla's

seat is one aisle over, in the front. Michael usually sits in the back of the room. His seat is empty, and I hope he's not absent today.

Rihanna has moved her chair over to Shayna's desk in the next row. She's not big on following rules. Shayna has her notebook on her lap and is copying something down. "Your handwriting is jacked up, Rihanna. Who taught you how to write? A monkey?" she says.

"You wouldn't have to worry about that if you did your own homework," Rihanna answers, yanking the book out of Shayna's hands.

"Whatever. Hey Dellie," Shayna whispers. "Let me see your math homework in case this whacked-out-looking dude asks for it."

"Yeah, b-but," I stutter. "I don't know if it's right or anything." I hand over my notebook.

"What're you thinking? You know Dellie can't do no math. You might as well just hand in a blank page," Rihanna says to Shayna, laughing. "You'll get a better mark."

My face gets hot.

"Yeah, I forgot. This girl doesn't even know what two plus two is," Shayna says, handing the notebook back to me. "He probably won't collect it anyway."

Michael rushes in just before the late bell rings, and I feel a little better. His hair bounces some in the wind he creates and my heart speeds up. He takes his time once he sees we have a sub.

Kayla looks over at me. "Ask him," she mouths.

I pretend not to understand her.

Michael has to walk past me to get to his seat. "Hey," he says.

The most I manage is a lame smile.

The sub finally stands up. He's big, and I wonder how his legs fit under the desk. He's holding the attendance sheet in his hand. "Time to get things started," he says.

The room gets quiet except for somebody popping their gum.

"My name is Mr. Dumbrewski, and . . ."

Laughter starts up like he's just told a joke and *Dumbrewski* is the punch line.

"Yo, that name is so messed up," Rihanna says.

Xavier, this Dominican kid, laughs like it's the funniest thing he's ever heard. "You should slap your father for giving you that name," he says.

"Dumb*who*?" Shayna asks.

I cover my mouth so a giggle doesn't sneak out. Kayla's doing the same thing at the front of the room.

Alexa hesitates outside the door before coming in. She probably thinks this is the wrong classroom.

"Do you belong in this class?" Mr. Dumbrewski asks.

"Yeah," Alexa answers. "This is Mrs. Robertson's class, right?"

"Yes, it is and since I haven't taken attendance yet,

you don't need a late pass. But keep in mind, I don't like interruptions."

"Whatever," Alexa says, slowly walking to her seat.

Mr. Dumbrewski clears his throat. "Before you think your jokes about my name are clever and witty, let me tell you this." He's not yelling, but his voice is strong and everybody shuts up. "I've heard them all before. They're old, tired, and dry." He rubs his chin. "Kind of like some of your math grades."

Things have stopped being funny. Maybe he's talking about my math grades.

"That's cold," somebody whispers.

"Now, in case you Einsteins haven't noticed," Mr. Dumbrewski continues, "Mrs. Robertson is out today. I'm not sure when she'll be back and until she decides to grace you all with her mathematical brilliance, I'll be your teacher. Please pass your homework up."

"Great," Shayna says to herself.

After everyone does what they're told, the room gets quiet again. I hear the clock above the blackboard ticking. Mr. Dumbrewski looks us over and nods. "And since it seems there is to be a test today," he says, "put your notebooks away and let's get started, shall we?"

So much for an extra study day.

SIX

Kayla has to run some errands for her mother, so I'll have to walk home from school alone.

A bunch of kids are trying to get out the door at once and it looks more like an escape than dismissal time.

I hang back and watch Kayla as she squeezes herself through the crowd.

Suddenly Michael is standing next to me, looking nervous. "Hey Dellie, what's up?"

My heart pounds like crazy again. "Nothing."

The crowd has thinned out and when we get to the door, he holds it open for me. I accidentally brush up against him as I pass. Being so close to Michael makes me nervous and happy at the same time. I've never felt like this before.

"How do you think you did on the test?" he asks, walking with me to the corner.

I lie. "Good, great."

"Yeah, me too. It was easy."

Rihanna and Shayna do a double take when they pass us. "Check out the romance," Shayna says.

"Don't do anything I wouldn't do," Rihanna says, laughing so hard she can barely get it out.

"Those two are really stupid," Michael says when they've moved ahead of us.

"Yeah," I agree.

"My bus is coming. I guess I'll see you tomorrow." He looks down the street. "Maybe we can walk together again after school?"

My face hurts from smiling too much. Wait until Kayla hears about this. "Okay," I answer.

"Cool." He steps on the bus.

Tomorrow can't come fast enough for me. My smile stays in place the rest of the way home.

Corey is playing alone in the courtyard when I get home. Some other kids are running around him like he's not there.

In the projects, you're never really alone when you're outside. You might be by yourself, but you won't be alone. My mother doesn't want to hear that, though.

We don't live on a block where all the buildings neatly line up. Each building has five floors and every one looks exactly the same. Three of them form our courtyard. A huge tree used to stand outside my building but the city-housing people chopped it down to make room for basketball hoops. I guess they thought we didn't like shade.

A few benches are set up in the middle of the courtyard. The paint is peeling off them and if you sit there too long when the weather is hot, you get tiny flakes of blue paint stuck to your butt.

Different groups of people are always sitting on the benches, especially when it's warm, like now. Old people sit on the benches closest to my building and teenagers sit on the ones farthest from the old people. Sometimes the teenagers get too loud and the old people have to shush them, especially if it's summertime, when they hang out way after everyone else has gone to bed.

Usually, I watch the courtyard from my bedroom window. My elbows get sore and red from leaning on the windowsill so much. Every now and then, Kayla and some of the other girls wave up to me on their way to the playground. I can't get mad at Kayla for playing outside without me. It's not her fault I'm a prisoner.

The kids running around Corey catch my attention. They're red, sweaty and happy. They're screaming and laughing like maniacs just like Louis used to when he was playing.

You can tell summer's coming because the teenagers have their music going already and some of them are dancing.

One of the old people, Mr. Brown, is also sitting in the courtyard. He's wearing his hat. It's a Kangol, like the one

Samuel L. Jackson wears. I've never seen him without it.

Everybody seems worry-free today but sometimes people around here do have things to worry about, like Ernest, a kid who lives in Alexa's building. His mother went to jail for selling clothes she stole from a department store. People call it boosting. They can call it what they want; it's still stealing.

My parents moved here when they got married. They say it was much nicer back then. They never had to worry about thieves or gunshots.

I don't know what it's like to live in a different place. I wonder how it would feel to live in a house with a bedroom big enough for a huge bed I can stretch out in without my arm hanging over the side.

The people who live here are poor, but for different reasons. Not everybody knows that. They think we're all the same. But that's not true. Some people spend their money on drugs and beer. Others, like my parents, are just working poor. My father drives a forklift all day and my mother works in a clothing factory packing up store orders. They go to work every day but don't get paid much. My father says he'll sell his soul if that's what it'll take for me to go to college.

Kayla and her mother lived in a big building with a doorman before her mother lost her job on Wall Street. One day after school, Kayla came home to find people buying up all her favorite things, including the bracelet her father gave her before he left them. After a while, they couldn't afford to stay in that fancy building because her mother couldn't find another job right away.

When Kayla told me her mother said it killed her to move here with people like us, I didn't know what she meant.

"She thought everybody who lived here was a lowlife with no class," Kayla explained. Hearing that was like being kicked. It felt horrible knowing some people see my parents that way.

Then Kayla made me swear I wouldn't tell anybody at school how she used to take piano lessons and art classes but can't now since she's poor. She said they didn't need to know all her business.

"Come on, you're not *that* poor. You've got more than some people," I said, pointing to her iPod. "And I wish I had your clothes. They're way better than mine."

"Yeah, but my mother's just temping at a bank now. She doesn't get paid as much as she did at her old job," she answered. "She doesn't even get a paid vacation."

"At least she has a job," I said.

"You don't understand what it's like to have so much one day and hardly anything the next."

I couldn't argue with that. She's right. I have no idea what it's like to have more than I need.

As I walk by, Corey moves away from the mound of dirt he's piling up. "Hi, Dellie, do you have something for me to eat?" he whispers.

He's wearing a pair of shorts. His knees are dirty. I open my backpack to find one of the free mints my father brings me from the diner he stops by every morning. I hold it out to Corey.

"This is all I have in my bag, but if you're really hungry, come upstairs with me. I'll make you a sandwich or something."

I must've said it too loud because some of the other kids look over at us. Instead of reaching out for the candy, Corey shakes his head like he's changed his mind.

"I'm sorry," I say in a lower voice, holding the candy in my open palm. "Please, take it."

"Cut it out, Dellie," Kayla says from behind me.

I'm surprised to see her so soon.

"You're embarrassing him," she says under her breath.

"I know. I didn't mean to."

Corey sits on the ground with his back to me. I kneel next to him and quietly sneak the mint candy into his hand. "I'm really sorry I embarrassed you," I say, holding on a few seconds longer than necessary. "Come upstairs later, okay?"

He nods, stuffing the candy into his mouth.

Kayla leans over and palms his head like it's a basketball and gives him a pack of bubble gum. "Thanks!" Corey says, getting up to play.

"Guess who walked with me after school today," I say to Kayla as we head toward our building.

Her eyes get big. "Don't tell me! Was it Michael?"

"Yes! He even held the door open for me and I kind of brushed against him by accident."

"Are you serious?" she asks.

"Yeah, and he asked me if we can walk together after school again."

"Didn't I tell you he likes you?" Kayla says, pushing on my arm.

Miss Etta and Miss Liz walk by us with their shopping carts just then. They've been friends forever. I never see just one of them. They're always together. Some people think they're sisters even though they look nothing alike. Miss Liz is tall and wears glasses attached to a chain that hangs around her neck. She's always dressed up, even if she's just going to the check-cashing place. Miss Etta is short, even shorter than I am. She wears a housedress everywhere she goes and smells like Bengay.

"Hi, Miss Liz, Miss Etta," Kayla and I chirp.

"Hello, ladies. Had a good day at school?" Miss Etta asks before coughing and spitting into a flowered handkerchief. It's gross and I know I should be used to it by now, but I'm not.

Kayla says it was good, but I say it was great, thinking about Michael.

"That's wonderful. Study hard now, you hear?" Miss Liz says, giving us a toothless grin. Sometimes she has her teeth in and sometimes she doesn't. She looks better with them in. Then her lips don't look like she's sucking on lemons.

"Okay," we answer.

When they turn to walk away, Miss Etta bumps right into Corey's mother, who is dragging Corey behind her so fast he's having a hard time keeping up.

Corey's mother doesn't have any of the curves my mother or my aunts have. My mother promises that one day I'll have them too because it's in our blood. I hope she's right because I'm as straight and flat as my bedroom wall.

"Just 'cause you're old don't mean you don't have to watch where you're goin'," Corey's mother says.

This is the first time I've seen her up close. There's a wide, light brown scar in the middle of her forehead. It stands out against her dark skin.

"It's you who should watch where you're going," Miss Etta says. "Why don't you have some respect? And why on earth are you pulling your little boy around so hard?"

"Why don't you respect me and mind your own business?" She jerks Corey's arm again and points to me. "You," she says. "Don't be telling my son he can come to you if he's hungry. You think I'm neglectful," she says, as if she's insulted. "Like I don't feed him or something?"

Whatever happiness I was feeling about Michael is all gone now. "No, no. It wasn't like that . . ."

"Well, that's what he told me," she says, watching me

closely. "You telling me he's lying? 'Cause if you are, we got a whole new set of problems that need fixing, don't we, Corey?"

"Nooo, Mama," he says, shaking his head fast. "I'm not lying. She did say it."

My legs feel weak and hotter than the rest of my body. "He's telling the truth," I say.

"Now, you said what you had to say," Miss Etta interrupts. "So, why don't you move on?"

"How many times do I have to tell you?" Corey's mother sounds like she's getting ready to teach a dog a lesson. "This business is not your business."

Miss Liz grabs Miss Etta's arm. "Let's go." She looks nervously toward our building. "You don't know if she's carrying a gun or not," she says. "You too, girls. Go on."

"That's right." Corey's mother laughs. "You-all get out of my face."

"I feel so bad for Corey," Kayla says as we get closer to our building. "What's wrong with his mother? Why is she so mean?"

"She just is," I answer, feeling sick. "And I'm not going to stop feeding him no matter what she says."

"What if she finds out?" Kayla asks. "You see how nasty she was. Who knows what she's capable of?"

She's right, but there's no way I'm going to stop helping

Corey. I just can't. Maybe I can change things for him somehow even if I can't change anything for me.

All of a sudden, two guys start arguing near one of the benches. They're standing so close to each other I don't know how they can breathe. Corey's mother walks over to them like they're not about to start swinging their fists.

"You better back up off me if you know what's good 'cause I got something for you," one of the guys says, reaching into his pocket.

"What if he has a gun? What if he was the one who put the bullet in Corey's door?" I ask Kayla.

"Let's not hang around to find out," she answers.

We're almost on the steps of our building when one of the guys hits the other so hard, blood flies from his mouth.

Corey's mother is in the mix now. "Hit him back." She's jumping up and down. "Beat his stupid behind."

"Girls, get inside!" Mr. Brown yells out to us.

He doesn't have to tell us twice. We hurry up the steps.

"You have some time before your parents get home. Come up to my apartment," Kayla says when we get to my floor.

Once safe in Kayla's bedroom, we peek out the window. The benches have emptied and there's no sign of the guys who were fighting.

"How crazy was all that?" Kayla says.

"Which part? Corey's mother or those guys?"

"The guys were pretty bad, but what about Corey's mother? She was way worse. I don't think you should feed him anymore," Kayla says. "She wasn't playing."

If Louis was hungry, I'd want somebody to feed him. "He's just a little kid." I try to fight off the tightening in my throat. "It's not right."

"What's going on in here?" Kayla's mother says, standing in the doorway.

"Mom!" Kayla spins around. "I didn't know you were home."

"I can see that." Her mom walks over to look out the window too. Her high heels click across the floor. "Have your manners fallen out the window, Dellie?" she asks, looking at me sideways.

"Hi, Ms. Warren."

"That's better." Her lips pull into a tight line and I wonder if she thinks I'm a lowlife too. "Kayla, you may have a quick snack, then promptly move on to your homework." Then she clicks her way out of the room. She sounds worse than a teacher.

After dinner later, my mother quietly goes into Louis's room and closes the door.

"Please clean up, Dellie," my father says, going in after her. At first there's only whispering, but then my mother's crying fills the air. I busy myself at the kitchen sink so I won't hear any more.

I go to bed early and dream of a baby lying in a crib. Cows and elephants hang from a mobile above. It turns slowly as a lullaby plays softly. The room is bright at first, but as I walk farther in, the light dims until the only thing I can see is the baby, who is kicking its chubby legs and smiling a big, gummy smile.

"Hi, baby," I say, reaching for its soft hand. "I'll take care of you, don't worry."

I bend over to kiss him. I smell baby lotion and hum along with the lullaby. The baby laughs.

But somebody calls me outside to play. I'm jumping rope with some girls I don't know when Kayla appears.

"Dellie! Where's the baby?"

Panic washes over me. I rush back to the crib, but the only thing in it is a stuffed animal. When I turn it over, I realize it's Connie Boy.

My pillow is sweaty and my hair is stuck to the back of my neck when I wake up. My heart is racing and my breathing comes in short bursts. The panic has followed me. I put the pillow over my face and sob into it until there's nothing left.

SEVEN

I sometimes go to the grocery store with my mother on Saturday mornings. It's usually uneventful, but this morning is different.

While we wait for the elevator with a shopping cart full of groceries, the door to Corey's apartment flies wide open. It scares my mother so much, she drops the handle of the cart and it falls over. Instead of picking it up, she stands in front of me.

My legs get weak and hot again, just like when Corey's mother accused me of thinking she was neglectful.

The guy who got punched the other day comes out of the apartment. Corey's mother is with him. She's mad and cursing. I can't believe she's only wearing her underwear, a T-shirt and socks.

The man lifts his hand like he's going to hit her. "No!" she yells.

He laughs. It's drawn out and louder than it needs to be.

"That's right. You better remember that," he says before walking out of the building.

Corey's mother kicks a tomato that has fallen out of the cart. It hits the wall. It was fat and ripe and on sale. My mother was going to use it for tomorrow's salad and now it's smashed and dripping onto the floor.

"What ya looking at, huh?" Corey's mother says with clenched teeth before disappearing into her apartment.

We go upstairs and put the groceries away. The whole time, my mother mumbles to herself in Spanish.

When everything is put in its place, mom ties her hair in a ponytail. Then she takes a rag and a bottle of spray cleaner out from underneath the kitchen sink.

"Dellie," she says, handing me a roll of paper towels, "come downstairs with me. I want you to help me clean up that mess."

Corey's mother should be the one to clean it, since she's the one who made the mess, but I know she'd never do that.

We walk down the steps instead of taking the smelly elevator. Every now and then, if it's not broken, people pee in it. I guess they're too lazy to find a real bathroom. When that happens, my mother pours pine cleaner mixed with hot water onto the elevator floor to rinse it. When the water drains out, it goes down into the elevator shaft. The housing-maintenance guys complain about it, but my mother says too bad, it's better than having to stand in pee.

On the first floor, my mother begins to wipe away the guts of the tomato after I've sprayed it. The seeds have started to stick and she has to rub a little harder for them to come off.

"Qué desperdicio," my mother says as she works.

She's right, having the tomato smashed like that is a waste, even if it was on sale.

I stand in front of Corey's door and can't help but stare at the bullet hole. Underneath the red paint, the door is gray. It makes me think of blood and the bone under it. And that makes me think of Louis, but I shut down that part of my brain.

The only thing I hear coming from inside Corey's apartment is the television and I'm not sure if that's a good thing or not. I'd feel better if I at least heard his voice.

"Delilah, move away from there!" my mother hisses when she sees where I'm standing. I jump at the sound of her voice. "Give me the paper towels. Then go upstairs."

"Can't I wait for you on the stoop? You'll still be able to see me from there."

My mother hesitates at first but then says, "Okay. As long as you don't move out of my sight. And only until I'm finished."

The courtyard is starting to come alive and since it's so warm out, it'll be that way into the night.

Some kids are on their bicycles, and others are trying to

Rollerblade, but their ankles keep twisting and wobbling all over the place.

I've never Rollerbladed because my mother thinks I'll get hurt, but I think I'd be good at it. My father used to take me ice-skating all the time and I did fine. Louis watched from the side and whenever I managed to spin without falling, he'd yell, "Hooray for my supersister!"

Alexa waves to me from her stoop. She's lucky to be able to play outside so much.

Her light brown hair is parted in the middle, with two long braids hanging over her shoulders. "Hi, Dellie," she says, coming over to me. "You think your mother will let you go for a walk?"

"Let me ask," I say, even though I already know the answer.

Alexa follows me back inside. I wish she would've waited outside. I don't want her to see me beg for something she gets so easily.

"Mom, can I go for a walk with Alexa?"

My mother gives the wall one last wipe. "No," she answers, without looking up.

"But it's so nice out and I'll come right back. Please?"

She starts up the stairs. "What did I say, Delilah?"

I don't give her an answer because she doesn't wait for one.

"Maybe you should ask your father," Alexa whispers.

"When my father was around, he never said no to me. I had him wrapped around my little finger."

"He's not home. He's out fixing our car."

Alexa sucks on her teeth. "Why doesn't your mother ever let you play outside anyway?"

"It's because of, you know," I say before turning toward the stairs. "What happened last year."

"Oh." She looks at the spot my mother was wiping. "Why was she cleaning the hallway?"

"Because," I say, keeping my voice quiet, "Corey's crazy mother made a mess."

"Seems like she's always up to something." Alexa looks at the bullet hole in Corey's door. "I kind of feel sorry for that kid," she says, shaking her head.

"Me too," I say. "Somebody has to help him."

"You don't mean somebody like you?" she asks.

"Maybe. Why?" I also look at Corey's door. I wish I could just bust it down and take him away.

"What could *you* do?" She snickers. "You're never even allowed out."

"If I can get my father wrapped around my finger like you did yours, maybe that'll change."

"Say you do get out," Alexa says, crossing her arms against her chest. "What are you going to do to help Corey?"

It's a good question. Too bad I don't have an answer for it.

"Delilah?" my mother calls out before I can think of an answer for Alexa.

"Coming, Mom!" I say, running up the steps.

When I get up to my floor, Mrs. Lawrence is throwing her trash into the garbage chute. She's wearing a red dress that buttons down the middle, a pair of white ankle socks and slippers. She's got a scarf on her head and I see the bumps from her curlers underneath. My mother has already gone inside.

"Hi there, Dellie. How're you doing today?"

"Hi, Mrs. Lawrence. I'm fine."

"That's good to hear," she says, sticking her hands into the pockets of her dress.

I start to push my door open, but Mrs. Lawrence isn't finished talking yet. Sometimes she's like that. She doesn't work and since she's home all day, I guess she's lonely.

"I've been living in this building for a long time and I must say, we've been very lucky. It's been peaceful up till now." Mrs. Lawrence shakes her head. "But ever since the new people moved in on the first floor, things have changed. Bullet holes in doors, fighting, yelling. It's just shameful."

I don't know why she's telling me all this.

"Since you've been spending time with that little boy, feeding him and such," she continues, "I want you to be extra careful. When he knocks on my door, I give him something he can take with him. You should do the same."

"Sometimes I do too," I say, hoping my mother's not listening.

"Maybe you should do it all the time. You just don't know what his mother and her friends will do next." When she closes her door, I hear two regular locks and one chain lock slip into place.

In our apartment, my mother is dusting Louis's picture. I don't say anything about her red eyes or the tears she wipes away. "Do you want me to make you a sandwich?" she asks.

"Okay."

We eat in silence until my father comes home.

"Daddy!" I blurt out when I hear his key in the door.

"Please, Dellie," my mother says, holding her head. "Not so loud. I'm not feeling well."

After my mother goes into her bedroom and closes the door, I ask my father about going out. "I promise not to be gone too long," I say, kissing his scratchy cheek.

Even though it's Saturday and we all slept late this morning, my father's eyes look tired. I feel bad for trying Alexa's trick but not bad enough to let it go. He watches me for a few seconds before saying, "Did you ask your mother?"

He should be able to tell me yes right off the bat without having to get my mother's approval. It's so unfair.

"I did but she said no," I say, feeling desperate. "She didn't even think about it first, Dad!"

"I'll go in and talk to her."

"Thanks!" I hug him for trying.

I look out my bedroom window while I wait for my father to talk to my mother. Kayla's sitting on the bench. I call her name, but she doesn't look up. I call again, this time much louder, but there's still no answer and I wonder if she's ignoring me.

I busy myself with a daydream about Michael. If he lived around here, I'd see him all the time. Maybe we'd even walk to school together and he'd hold my hand or sneak a kiss in the hallway at school.

Those thoughts disappear when I see the look on my father's face. "But Dad!" I say, wondering why the trick didn't work.

"This is something that will take longer than a year, Dellie. Give your mother some more time."

My words slowly work their way into my mouth. "But I'm tired of waiting."

"I know, honey," he says, trying to hug me, but I don't let him.

My father leaves my room without another word. I rip a piece of paper out of my notebook and write a note to Kayla telling her about the trick and how bad it failed. I call to her again, hoping she'll answer me this time, but she doesn't, and I know she's definitely ignoring me.

I fold the paper up small, and just as I toss it out the window, Kayla gets up and leaves the courtyard. It's a good thing I didn't sign my name. The note twirls through the air like a helicopter. It has more freedom than I do.

EIGHT

Today, there's a moving truck parked on the sidewalk in front of my building. Usually people don't move in on a Sunday. Sundays are for church people and homework.

The moving men carry in all kinds of weird stuff, including a giant statue of an angel. It looks like something you'd see in the cemetery. It takes two guys to carry it, three if you count the guy holding the door open and telling the other two where to step.

I count five kitchen chairs. Each one is painted a different color. One is black with gold stars, one is hot pink, one is green like a Granny Smith apple, one is sky blue with white spots on it and the other one is tangerine-y orange.

When the movers come to my floor, I know the new people must be moving into Mr. Millson's apartment, right next to the elevator.

Mr. Millson was older than any other person in my building. He was a small man with hardly any hair. He reminded me of a baby chick. His dark brown eyes were rimmed in blue and when he wore his thick glasses his eyes looked like big, wet marbles. You could hear his slippers rub against the floor as he shuffled around in his apartment. Not actual footsteps, just sliding noises.

After Louis died, Mr. Millson started knocking on our door to ask my mother if I could read the newspaper to him. He didn't really want to hear what was going on in the world because he'd fall asleep as soon as I began to read. But the minute I stopped, he'd wake up like he'd heard an alarm clock going off. It didn't matter to me, though. It was good to be out of my apartment and he probably knew it. Sometimes I'd read the paper twice just so I could stay longer.

When Mr. Millson's son walked him out of the building for the last time, I waved good-bye from my open window, hoping he'd see me, but he never did.

I peer through the peephole, trying to get a look at my new neighbors.

The elevator door opens and a tall woman steps out. She doesn't seem old but it's hard to see clearly.

She's wearing a long, purple cape. It's fastened at the neck with a big, gold button. The sides of the cape flow behind her. If I didn't know any better, I'd think she was a witch.

She's wearing a black and gold turban on her head. Long braids hang out the sides. She's using a cane almost as big as I am and bells jingle every time she takes a step.

I grab the phone and dial Kayla's number. Her mother picks up and asks me to wait a few seconds. Then her mother's back, telling me Kayla's not home. I don't believe her. Kayla's never been this mad at me before and I have no idea what I could have done.

It's not right to spy, but I'm bored and with Kayla not talking to me it's all I have to do. Cape Woman stands in front of Mr. Millson's door with one hand open like she's expecting something to be put into it. Then, she leans her head back a little. I hear mumbling but can't make out what she's saying. When she's done, she kisses her hand and places it on the door.

I'm getting tired of holding the peephole lid open so I let it fall, and accidentally hit the doorknob. When I peek out again, Cape Woman's looking in my direction, nodding like she's answering a question. I back away only to hear a light knocking.

Staying home alone has its advantages, like watching whatever I want on television, but right now, I'd trade in all my shows for having my parents here with me.

"Who is it?" I call out, trying to sound like somebody older. Somebody with attitude. I wish Kayla had gotten on the phone.

"Hello. I am Miss Shirley," she says too loudly in a Jamaican accent. I guess she's making sure I hear her through the steel of the door. "I'm just now moving in next door," she adds.

"Oh, hi," I return, not sure what to say, but I know I'm not opening the door.

Miss Shirley doesn't say anything back right away. Then I hear, "Okay, well, I can come back another day." This time she's not so loud. "I'd like to ask you a couple of *tings*."

"That's fine," I say.

She must be walking back to Mr. Millson's apartment because I hear the bells again but they're getting quieter.

I stand at the door and think about Mr. Millson and how I haven't been inside his apartment in such a long time. I wonder if it will still smell like him, not that he smelled bad. He just had his own smell. Like Ivory soap and peppermint mixed together.

Thinking about Mr. Millson's apartment almost makes me open the door. Almost.

NINE

I t's pouring like mad and rain on a Monday is never good. It makes me want to stay in bed and forget all about school, but then I think about Michael. No amount of rain can keep me from seeing him.

My mother is already at work and my father's in the bathroom, so I stand in front of Louis's picture and say a prayer to him. This time I ask him not to hate me. Then I remind him of how much I love him. I eat breakfast while hoping for Kayla's knock, but I finish my whole bowl of cereal plus my toast and still, no knock. No one answers her phone when I call to find out what the deal is either. I give up waiting and grab my backpack and umbrella. "Time to go, Dad."

"No Kayla today?" my father asks.

"I guess she's not going," I lie.

Outside, I see Alexa and she doesn't have her little sister with her.

"Hey, wait up!" I call.

She switches her umbrella to her other hand while she waits.

I jump over a huge puddle to catch up to her. I know by the time I get to school my feet will be soaked. "Where's your sister?"

"She was coughing all night and this morning she has a fever. My mother's staying home with the brat," she says. "Why aren't you walking to school with Kayla?"

I don't want her to know Kayla's mad at me. "Maybe she's sick too."

"No, she's not sick. I saw her leave."

"Maybe she was going to the doctor."

"I don't think so, Dellie. She had her backpack and her mother wasn't with her. Maybe she's mad at something you said about her."

"I would never say anything bad about her. Kayla's my best friend."

"*Was* your best friend," Alexa says.

"What are you talking about?" I'm starting to feel panicky, like I'm loosing someone else.

"You'll have to find out on your own," Alexa answers.

I shouldn't have to find out anything. I should already know. "She probably just had to be in school early for a makeup test, that's all." It sounds like I'm trying to convince myself.

"Whatever."

Alexa tries jumping over another puddle but lands in it

instead, drenching my pants. "Oops, sorry," she says, sounding like she doesn't mean it. "By the way, how's your get-out-of-jail-free card coming?" she asks, looking down the block to my dad.

"Oh, it's coming," I say.

The wind picks up and we have to fight to hold our umbrellas straight. "I heard you were walking with Michael," she says. "You think he's cute?"

"Kind of."

"Yeah, me too," Alexa smooths down her long hair. "I think he likes me."

My face is burning up. "Really?" I ask, slowing down.

"Yeah, I caught him looking at me a couple of times. Oh, and when I was *out* yesterday, I went Down the Back to see where he lives." We call it Down the Back because it's at the very end of our neighborhood, near the water. It's still a part of our neighborhood, but it has real houses, not tall, brick project buildings.

"How do you know he lives there?" I ask, feeling stupid for not knowing something else I should.

"It was easy. I asked around. It's not like it's a secret or anything. And," she says, spinning her umbrella, "I'm thinking about going there later and if he's outside, maybe we'll do something together. *Or*, I could just ask him to hang out with me when I get to school." With that she takes off ahead of me.

The wind kicks up again and I don't bother trying to hold my umbrella straight. I close it up and race after her to school. If she's going to ask, I don't want to miss his answer. I hope my father can keep up.

When I get into homeroom, Kayla's already there.

"I told you," Alexa sings.

"What's up? Why didn't you come get me this morning?" I ask Kayla.

She keeps her eyes on the book she's reading. "Oh, I forgot."

"How can you forget? We always walk together."

"I said," Kayla snarls, turning the page roughly, "I forgot."

Having my best friend treat me like a dog makes me want to vomit. I quickly wipe the tears that spring into my eyes. I have to tell her I never said anything bad about her so she'll stop treating me like this. "Kay . . ."

"What?"

I take my seat without saying another word. I've never seen her this angry.

"Dellie," Alexa says, "you know you should leave that *poor* girl alone."

The rest of the kids laugh and I have no idea why until I think about how Alexa said the word *poor*. Then I understand. Kayla's secret is out.

"Stop laughing, it's not funny!" I say, but nobody listens.

In math class, Mr. Dumbrewski hands back our tests. "Very few of you did well on this exam," he says.

He places my test facedown. I let it sit there. I'm in no rush to see all those red *X*s.

"If you are one of those people, have no fear. I have a plan for getting you up to speed in time for your final exam, which takes place on June eighteenth. Please see me after class so that we can arrange tutoring sessions."

"What, like after school?" Xavier asks.

"After school, before school, whichever works the best."

"Yeah, right."

"And why is that?" Mr. Dumbrewski asks.

"Man," Xavier says. "'Cause being in school when you don't have to be is lame."

"Are you one of those people who need extra help in math, Xavier?"

"No! I'm not stupid."

I peel back the corner of my test until I see a circle drawn at the top of the paper. A 57. I did better than last time.

"I'm not stupid either!" Rihanna says.

In front of me, Shayna tips back in her chair. "Shoot, me neither!" she says, pushing against my desk.

"Not me!" Alexa calls out. She's waving her test like a flag. She got a 91. I guess if I ever got a ninety-anything, I'd show off too.

Xavier lets out a small groan. "Not me, not me," he mimics in a high-pitched voice.

"Shut up," Alexa says. "You're just jealous!"

"Enough!" Mr. Dumbrewski says. "This has nothing to do with being stupid. Everyone in this room is more than capable of passing."

I guess he hasn't gotten a really good look at my track record yet.

When class is over, I think about talking to Mr. Dumbrewski, but Michael and Alexa are standing by his desk. I hope Alexa hasn't asked Michael anything yet.

When I walk past, Alexa stops me. "What did you get, Dellie?"

My face warms up. I look for Kayla but she's gone. "Get for what?"

"Duh, your math test. I got a ninety-one but Michael beat me." She pushes on his shoulder and giggles like an idiot. "He got a ninety-six. We're going to be tutors."

I hope being tutored isn't something Mr. Dumbrewski says I have to do.

"It's not such a big deal," Michael sighs. "I studied, that's all."

"It is a big deal," Mr. Dumbrewski says. "You should be proud." His voice is powerful and he sounds like he's talking about something more important, like protecting the ozone layer, rather than a seventh-grade math test.

Alexa takes a piece of her hair and twirls it around her

finger, trying to look cute. "Mr. Dumbrewski is right. You're smart, Michael. Probably the smartest one in the whole class."

"I have to go," I say, walking away.

Michael grabs his books off Mr. Dumbrewski's desk. "Wait up, Dellie. I'll walk with you."

Suddenly I'm happier than if I'd gotten 100 on my test. "Okay," I say, holding the door for him.

"No, Michael. You can't go," Alexa says quickly. "Mr. Dumbrewski is about to tell us the tutoring details. Right, Mr. Dumbrewski?"

"We'll get it settled after lunch. Go to your next class before you're late," he answers.

"Michael," Alexa blurts out. "Wait. I have to ask you something."

"Not now," Michael says.

"Desperate much?" I say to Alexa before stepping into the hallway with Michael.

I try to get Kayla's attention in every class we have together, but she ignores me. I know why she's upset. I'm just not sure what it has to do with me. I didn't do anything.

When the bell rings at the end of the day, Kayla is nowhere around. It's still raining, so I open my umbrella.

"Hey, can I share with you? I forgot to take mine this morning."

Michael hunches himself under my umbrella. He looks funny bent over and I try to hold the umbrella up higher for him. "Okay, sure. No problem." I notice how long his eyelashes are and a hot feeling starts in my stomach and works its way to my head.

"Cool," he says.

We only walk a few feet before Alexa runs out the door and stops us. "Don't forget about tonight, Michael. My house at eight. We have to have the tutoring schedules made up and back to Mr. Dumbrewski by tomorrow," she says.

The static from my umbrella is making stray pieces of Michael's hair stand on end. "How can I forget?" he says. "You've been reminding me all day."

"I'm just making sure," Alexa says. "Dellie, you never told me what you got on the math test. Did you pass?"

The way she stretches out the word *you* makes it sound suspicious. Like she already knows what the answer is. I ignore her and we leave her behind.

"I think the tutoring thing went to her head," Michael says just as a gust of wind shakes the umbrella. My heart almost bursts when he puts his hand over mine to help me hold it.

Michael's bus is already at the corner when we get there. He digs his bus pass out of his pocket. "Maybe I'll stop by to see you tonight before I go to Alexa's. You live in the building opposite from hers, right?" he says running up the bus steps. "Be near the benches around seven-thirty."

Alexa won't like that one bit, but I sure do. My pulse races. I nod but I'm not sure he can see me. I've pulled the umbrella down over my face. There's no way my mother is going to let me have a boy over. It's good pretending she would, though.

I've forgotten about tutoring, and about Alexa and Kayla. All I think of the whole way home is how warm Michael's hand felt against mine.

Being home alone on rainy days is different from when the sun is shining, especially now that it's thundering and lightning. Days like this used to scare Louis, so I'd play games with him to distract him from the weather.

Somewhere in the building there is shouting.

"Mommy, please let me back in!"

It's Corey. I unlock our door and step into the hallway. I'm breaking a major rule by leaving the apartment, but I can't help it. Corey needs help, my help.

I lean over the railing and look down one flight into the stairwell. I don't see anything, so I slowly creep down the steps.

On the first floor, Corey is sitting in front of his apartment door. His head is buried in his knees. The only thing he's wearing is a pair of ripped superhero pajama pants. His tiny ribs are heaving with every sob, not a cry. Crying can be done quietly. It can be done without anyone knowing.

My parents sobbed at Louis's funeral, but now, they just cry silently. "Louis," I whisper. "Are you okay?"

He lifts his head but doesn't answer.

"Louis, what's wrong?" I ask.

"Louis?" He wipes his nose on his arm. "Who's Louis, Dellie?" he asks.

"What?"

"You called me Louis."

I don't know what to say.

"Nobody. I just made a mistake."

I've never made that mistake before and it scares me. It scares me even more that I said Louis was nobody. I could've said something other than nobody. I should have said Louis was my brother. I want it to echo off the walls so that everyone will hear it. I take a deep breath to stop the panic from swelling up but it comes anyway, like an unstoppable train.

"Dellie . . . Dellie, can you hear me?"

"Of course. I always hear you," I say focusing in on Corey.

"I know. That's why I like you so much." His eyes are clearer.

Without warning, Corey's apartment door opens and crashes into the wall. Corey waves as he goes inside.

I don't move for a long time. I listen to make sure everything's okay.

. . .

Back on my floor, I hear the bells.

"Hello," Cape Woman says.

"Hi," I say, staying close to my door.

"I'm Miss Shirley. I moved in yesterday."

"Yes, I know. I'm Dellie," I say, taking a quick look at her from her feet on up.

Even though summer is still a couple of weeks away, she's wearing sandals. Her toenail polish makes her toes look like they've been dipped in blood. Her eyes are ringed with black eyeliner and there is a mole on one side of her mouth. Her cheeks and lips are colored pink and make her look like a doll at the toy store. Small bells, like the ones some people attach to the laces of baby shoes, are hanging from her cane. I wonder what Kayla thinks about her.

"Can you tell me if there is somebody around here to go shopping for me today? I need to buy some grocery *tings* and my legs are aching," she says, hitting the floor with the end of her cane. The bells dance and make music.

I like how she says *things*. It sounds softer her way. *"Tings,"* I repeat without thinking.

Her bold laugh comes quick. Her whole body is involved. "Oh, girl," she says. "You like how I speak?"

Miss Shirley smiles with a wide mouth. She has straight,

shiny white teeth, like people in magazines have. Not like mine, which look too big for my mouth. My father keeps telling me that I'll grow into them. I hope he's right.

"Yes," I answer, embarrassed about repeating her.

I don't really know anyone from Jamaica. I've only heard Miss Shirley's accent on the bus and on TV commercials. "Is Jamaica really beautiful?" I ask.

"Yes, it is. And I miss it dearly even after all these years," she says. "But when I try hard enough, I can smell the sweet flowers or see the great mountains and the lovely turquoise sea."

I watch Miss Shirley as she talks, but I've stopped listening. She looks more than happy, but joyful, like she's not standing in a building with bullet-hole doors and hungry people living behind them.

"So, will you?" Miss Shirley is asking me.

I tune back in. "Will I what?" I ask.

"Go to the store for me?"

"Oh. Well, I can't right now. Maybe I'll be able to go later, if my mom says it's okay."

"Yes," Miss Shirley says, making the *s* hiss like snakes. "That will work out just fine. Why don't you come inside so I can give you a list of the *tings* I'm needin', just in case?"

I don't know if I should. It'd be easier to decide if Kayla was with me. I look over at Miss Shirley's apartment and she looks too. "It's good that you are cautious," she says, pointing to the open door of her apartment. "I will leave it just as it is."

Her door is held open by the black chair with the gold stars. I hear music playing softly. Lots of piano and maybe a trumpet.

There's a kid who lives around the corner who's in the school band. He plays the trumpet and gets teased so much I don't know how he hasn't quit yet. They call him Blowfish because when he blows into that thing, his cheeks stretch out far and round and he looks just like a blowfish on a hook. That kind of music never plays in my building. "Okay," I answer.

When I follow Miss Shirley into her apartment, she leaves the door propped open just like she said. Even though there's no hint of Mr. Millson, being here reminds me of Louis.

It feels like something prickly is trying to make its way down my throat, so I swallow hard, pressing it into the place I keep all my bad feelings. Only now, there doesn't seem to be much room left and I'm not sure what I'll do when it's filled up.

TEN

Miss Shirley pulls out the hot pink chair for me and I sit down.

There's a loaf of delicious-looking bread on the table. Miss Shirley sees me staring.

"I make a mean banana bread. And it's still warm," she says, cutting a thick slice for me.

I want to be polite and say no thank you, especially because I don't know Miss Shirley. She could've put something crazy in it. But when she slices a piece of bread for herself and takes a bite, I change my mind and start with a small piece.

It doesn't taste like regular bread. It's sweet and has lots of cinnamon, walnuts and banana in it.

"Mmm, this is delicious."

"Glad you like it. Help yourself to another piece. No need to be shy around me," she says while writing out her store list. The giant angel is standing in the corner watching me.

"See there," Miss Shirley says, pointing to an old black-

and-white photo of two young girls, as though I had asked about them.

One of the girls is around thirteen and the other is younger, maybe seven. The older girl is wearing a hat with long feathers sticking straight up. Bracelets travel all the way up her arm and her dress is long and puffy. I bet that one is Miss Shirley. The smaller girl is wearing a plain dress with a bow around her waist and one in her hair.

The little girl in the picture is grinning like she's trying to hold her laughter in. Almost like the person taking the picture was making a funny face or telling a joke. The older girl's smile is bold and wide. She's not trying to hide anything.

"The one on the right is my only sister, Aggie. She was the youngest," Miss Shirley says. "God rest her soul. I miss her more than any*ting*." She sighs. "And the other is me. We used to have such a good time together, me and Aggie. We were best friends."

"Your sister was pretty. I, uh, mean is pretty." I confuse myself. I guess she's dead, but I don't want it to sound like she isn't pretty anymore.

Miss Shirley laughs. "Yes, she was very pretty." She points to another frame. The woman in it is not ugly or pretty, just really old. "And this is my mother."

I look at the other pictures on the table. They're all old. I don't see any rosary beads or candles like in my house.

"This is all I have left of my people," Miss Shirley

announces. She doesn't sound sad, just like she's stating a fact. Like it's raining today, or she's hungry.

I don't need to know what happened to her sister. I know people just aren't around forever.

"Do you have any siblings, Dellie?"

I jump at her question and a piece of bread gets sucked down my throat. Miss Shirley pours me a glass of milk when I start to cough.

I take a long drink, hoping she'll forget the question.

It must've worked because she doesn't ask again, but that doesn't stop my eyes from tearing up.

"Dellie, what has got you feeling so sad?"

"Oh, I'm not sad." I sniffle. "I have allergies, that's all," I say, looking at everything except Miss Shirley.

Miss Shirley goes to the bathroom to get a box of tissues. "For your allergies."

"Thank you." I take two.

While I wipe my eyes, I notice Miss Shirley's done a good job decorating Mr. Millson's apartment, except for the giant half-moon painted on the wall behind the kitchen table. It seems weird not to just have a picture of it in a frame hanging on the wall.

Miss Shirley follows my eyes to the moon. "Ah, yes, do you like that moon? It is my favorite *ting*, you know," she says, handing me the list.

"Why is it a half and not a whole?" I ask, glad for the conversation change.

"I'm pleased you had mind enough to ask," Miss Shirley says. She walks over to the moon and uses her finger to trace where the other half should be. "Just because we cannot see this half of the moon doesn't mean it's not there," she says, studying me. "We know this without having to actually see it." She points to her eyes. Her fingernails are sparkly gold. "You have to believe it's there. Faith, young one," she says, balling up her fist, "is powerful."

"Oh," I say. It seems simple now that she's explained it. "I see what you mean."

"I'm glad you know what I'm talking about," Miss Shirley says, smiling big.

I want to believe, but it's hard to believe something you can't see with your eyes. My mother wouldn't believe Louis was gone until she saw him. When she did, she screamed so loudly, I crawled behind a row of chairs in the emergency waiting room to hide from the sound. Nobody looked for me until hours later and I was glad.

Miss Shirley cuts another piece of banana bread and wraps it in tinfoil.

"Mrs. Lawrence tells me you feed the little boy who lives downstairs from time to time. Take this to him."

I bet Corey is going to love it.

"You know, Dellie, you're doing a very kind and considerate *ting* for Corey. Feeding food to those who are hungry is a good *ting*, a very good *ting*," she says, pulling dollars out of her wallet. "But feeding love to those who need it the most is even better. You can't buy that kind of nourishment in a store."

"Lots of people feed Corey," I say, making sure not to call him Louis again.

"Never minus points from your good deeds. There are plenty of people in this world who will do that for you. That little boy must believe in you, Dellie, because he comes to you knowing he'll get more than food."

I don't want Corey believing in me so much. I just thought maybe I could help him with his mother, but now I don't know. It feels like a lot of responsibility.

I'm tired of talking. I didn't come here to talk, talk, talk. Now I want to leave. "He shouldn't believe in me," I whisper.

"I'm sorry. I didn't hear what you said. These ears are starting to be disloyal to me."

"I *said*, he shouldn't believe in me. Nobody should." I stand up. Some crumbs fall from my lap to the floor, along with Corey's bread. I think about picking up the foil package, but I don't.

"And why is that, Miss Dellie?" Miss Shirley asks. Concern is etched across her face.

"Because." The panic rises to my chest. "I might not always be there to help him. That's why. He needs somebody else, somebody who'll always know what to do." I walk toward the door. "And I don't want to go shopping for you. You'll have to find somebody else. I shouldn't even be in here." I feel bad since she was so nice to me, but I can't stop myself.

I run out of Miss Shirley's apartment and into mine. I dial Kayla's number but lose my nerve and hang up before she can answer. She's not going to care about my problems now. Maybe not ever again.

Lying on my bed, I stare at the ceiling and think about Michael until my breathing calms down. He'll be here soon.

My parents come home an hour later than usual since they had an appointment with the therapist after work.

My mother's face is wet with tears. She doesn't say a word to me. She dusts Louis's picture, then goes to their bedroom and closes the door. There have been a lot of closed doors in my house since last year. Usually my mother does the closing.

My father's face is deeply creased. "Do you want something to eat?" I ask him.

"Sounds good, mami."

He has always called me that. He used to call my brother papi. To some people, that might sound strange, but in my family, those words mean love.

"I'll keep you company, okay?" my father says, sitting at the kitchen table. His words are slow, like he's thinking about something else.

"Okay," I say even though I think it's me who's keeping him company.

"What's new?" my father asks.

I think of telling him about Corey crying in the hallway earlier, but then I'll have to admit I broke a major rule by leaving the apartment when they weren't home. I don't dare tell him about Michael stopping by later or about me being a jerk and telling Miss Shirley I didn't want to go to the store for her.

"Nothing," I say.

"Kayla hasn't been around lately. Is she okay?" he asks.

"I don't know. She's not talking to me."

"Why?"

"She's mad at me."

"Well, good friends are hard to come by," he says, rubbing the back of his neck. "You should clear things up with her."

He's worn out and doesn't need to hear about my problem with Kayla, so I change the subject. "How about potatoes and eggs for dinner?"

"Sure, make whatever you want. It doesn't matter to me."

My father goes over to Louis's picture now too. He stands with his hand on the frame and closes his eyes. I know he's sending up a prayer just like I do, only he doesn't have to say he's sorry.

I make three plates of food. My father brings one of them

to my mother. He's still holding it when he comes back. He tries smiling, but it doesn't make it all the way to his eyes. "She's not hungry," he says.

My father picks through his own food. It doesn't seem like he's hungry either.

When we're done, we sit on the couch. My father puts his arm around me and I lay my head on his shoulder, curling up against him. "Will Mommy ever let me outside to play?" I ask, thinking about Michael.

"I'm sure she will," he says, staring toward their bedroom door. "Just give her some more time."

"What about you?" I ask, wiping the tears that have started down my cheeks. "Don't you need more time?"

"All I know is that life pushes on and you have to move with it. If you don't," he says, running his fingers through his short, graying hair, "you'll become stuck in a place where you didn't want to be to begin with."

"If that's true, then why doesn't Mom know it?"

"Deep down she does. She's just not ready to move yet. One day it'll happen. You'll see."

In a little while my father says, "How about a game of dominoes?"

"I'm not in the mood to play any games."

"Why?" he asks, taking out the dominoes tin. "Afraid you'll lose?"

"Yeah, right." I laugh. "How much do you want to bet I'll win?"

"Everything you got, of course."

It doesn't take long before my father beats me. He cackles evilly, then asks, "Who's your daddy?"

"Um, *you!*"

"I am. So. Lame." He laughs. "Want to play again?"

"No way."

After a while, my mother goes into the bathroom and runs the water. When she comes out, she's got a plastic smile on her face, like she picked it up out of a drawer and placed it over her real mouth. She sits in the rocking chair looking at my brother's picture as if it's going to tell her something.

Later, I write a note to Michael telling him that I can't come out. I put a smiley face next to my name. I read it and rip it up. It's too sloppy. I write it over four times until it looks okay. When it's ready, I fold it up tight.

At seven-fifteen, I watch for Michael from my bedroom window.

Alexa is coming back from the store. The bag she's carrying is so thin, it's see-through. She's got a large bag of Cheez Doodles and a bottle of iced tea. "For Michael," she says, looking up to the second floor. "They're his favorite."

I don't say anything, but secretly I wish she'd trip or something.

When Michael comes walking into the courtyard at seven-thirty, I wave my hand at him. "Pssst," I say.

When he comes closer, I throw my note to him. It seesaws its way down, but I duck behind my curtain before he reads it. I don't want to have to explain anything. Besides, he'll probably have a better time with Alexa. She's got Cheez Doodles and a mother who hasn't lost a son.

ELEVEN

'm having a good dream about Louis. My mother carries a cake over to the kitchen table. It's Louis's birthday.

"Make a wish," I tell him just before he blows out the candles.

"I wish for—," he starts.

"No, if you tell us it won't come true. Say it in your head," my mother explains.

He squishes his eyes shut. "Okay," he says, then blows out the flames. Smoke drifts into our faces.

"Yay!" We clap.

He puts some of the icing on my nose. I do the same to him. "Time for gifts!" he says.

My father puts a big box in front of Louis. I help Louis rip the shiny wrapping off. "I always wanted a train set," he says, getting up to kiss us.

. . .

"Dellie, Dellie, wake up, we've overslept."

My father is standing at my bedside. I should've washed some clothes when I noticed the hamper was full because he's wearing the work uniform with his name misspelled. Instead of *Alejandro* his name tag reads *Alejandog*. He only wears this one when his other ones are dirty. I hope the other forklift drivers are too busy to notice. It's been two days since my parents' last therapy session and my mother hasn't done any laundry because she's spending too much time being sad and staying in bed. Maybe she dreams of Louis and how he used to run around the house singing at the top of his lungs or how when he laughed hard, his curly hair bounced all over his head.

"Morning, Daddy," I say, sad to be awake.

"Good morning, mami. Get up or you'll be late for school," my father says, kissing my forehead. "Mommy isn't going to work today. She's still sleeping."

My father is unshaven and his eyes look droopy.

"Okay," I say.

I drag myself out of bed and get dressed. I remember that it's Wednesday, which means a double period of math first thing, so I walk slower.

My mother comes in while I'm brushing my teeth. Her eyes are red and swollen like she was crying all night instead of sleeping.

"Want to stay home from school today?" she asks.

She's never offered me a choice about school before and it's hard to decide. Yes, I want to stay home, but when my mother's like this, I know it'll be a day of quiet and sadness. Besides, if I go, I'll get to be around Michael.

I look at my mother in the mirror. "Nah, I think I'll go in. I don't want to have to do any makeup homework on top of all my other work."

She wipes away fresh tears. "I'll be able to sleep better knowing you're home safe today. I've already told your father to leave."

I know I shouldn't fight with her when she's like this. "Okay, I'll stay. Do you want some breakfast?"

"No, thanks, but wake me for lunch, okay? And remember, don't open the door for anybody."

I sit on the edge of the bathtub for a long time and think about when our family was normal. When there was more singing and less crying.

Louis's bedroom is exactly the way he left it. Connie Boy sits on top of his pillow, action figures are tucked inside a sneaker, train tracks lead to nowhere and little connecting building blocks are set up like a city. The bedsheets are the same too. Sometimes I see my mother lying across his bed and I know she's smelling them to remember.

Needing to remember too, I hold his favorite shirt to my nose.

I can see him in his pajamas. He's just out of the bath, powdered from head to toe. His hair is slicked back, parted on the side, and his face is scrubbed. He's dozing off next to me, holding Connie Boy.

This is the closest I'll ever get to Louis now. The thought hits me like it's new all over again and panic inches its way inside me. I suck in some air and slowly let it out my nose. "Please don't hate me," I whisper, letting my tears come.

In the kitchen, I turn the television on, but mute it. I like to watch people's faces without the sound. Louis and I always did this, only we'd put funny words in their mouths.

It's quiet while I eat, until a door slams somewhere in the building. There's nothing to see through the peephole, so I step into the hallway. Downstairs, Corey is crying again.

"Corey?" I whisper, walking down the steps.

He's sitting cross-legged on the floor in the middle of the hallway. He's wearing a pair of shorts and no shirt. There are five small black-and-blue marks on his arm and a fat red welt on his calf. I feel like my cereal might come back up.

He must be cold. These hallways will hold the coolness of the winter for at least a few more weeks. I take my sweater off and put it over his shoulders. He doesn't look up. I'm afraid of what he's going to look like when he does.

My hands are shaking and I don't know if it's because I'm mad that Corey is hurt or because I'm scared of his door opening.

"No, no," he answers, shaking his head from side to side. His nose is stuffed up and it makes his voice sound strange.

"What's happened?" I ask, putting my hand on his head. I forgot how little a five-year-old's head can be.

"My mama says I have to stay out here till her friends leave and I didn't want to 'cause I was watching TV." He lifts his head up slightly, just enough for me to see his red, swollen eyes. "So, I got beat."

From inside his apartment, I hear loud music and his mother's laughter.

He flinches when I gently touch the welt on his leg. "Your mother did this to you?"

He doesn't answer me but he doesn't have to.

The apartment door suddenly swings open and I jump back. Corey's mother steps out. Behind her is one of the guys who was fighting the other day. He's wearing clothes much bigger than he is. Next to him is a woman with wild hair who can't seem to hold herself up.

"Boy, go on into the house and wait for me to get back," Corey's mother says, ignoring me. "And if you know what's good for you, you won't be bringing nobody in with you."

"Okay, but when are you coming back?" Corey asks quietly.

The wild-haired lady claps her hands and laughs like she's just heard the funniest joke.

"Shut up, Nessa," Corey's mother says.

The guy nudges Corey's mother hard with his elbow. "Let's go."

"Don't worry about when I'll be back," Corey's mother finally answers.

"Okay." Corey wipes his eyes.

"And remember," she says, setting her eyes on me, "nobody but you." Then she and her friends are out of sight.

Anything could happen to a little boy home alone. I ask if he wants to come up to my apartment. My mother usually sleeps deep and I know she won't even know he's with me.

"No, my mama's coming right back," Corey says.

I know she's not coming back anytime soon. "But aren't you cold sitting here with hardly nothing on?" Louis hated being cold. He didn't even want to play in the snow. He'd rather watch from the window as I made snow angels for him.

"Yeah, a little," he says, standing up. "I'll get dressed and wait inside." Before Corey opens the door, he puts his finger up to the bullet hole and traces it. "You know who did this, Dellie?"

I shake my head.

"My mama said it was somebody trying to scare her friend Kendal. It didn't scare him, but it scared me. It was loud and

Mama screamed. Kendal smacked her right in her face and then I hid in the bathtub. I didn't want him to do that to me too." Corey takes his hand away from the door and I know he's afraid. "Can you come inside with me, Dellie?"

"I can't. You heard what your mother said."

"Please," he says. "Just until I get changed."

"Do you promise to be really quick?"

Corey nods.

I give in, wishing again that Kayla was with me so I wouldn't have to do this alone.

I follow him into his apartment. Just like the rest of the apartments, the floor is tiled with big, light brown squares, except Corey's are dirty and look more dark brown. In the living room there is only a small table covered with soda cans and empty food containers, a grimy chair with the stuffing coming out of the arms and a small television on the floor. In the kitchen the refrigerator door is open. A jar of mayonnaise with its cap missing sits on the top shelf next to a box of crackers. There are roaches in the sink and that almost makes me scream.

"I'll be right back. Don't worry, I won't take long," Corey says, disappearing into the bedroom.

I stand in the middle of the living room not touching a thing. I gather my hair together, twist it and shove it into the back of my shirt. I'm afraid a roach or something might get into it and I won't know until it's way too late.

In the bedroom where Corey is pulling a shirt over his head there is a bare mattress on the floor. The window shade is ripped and pulled down almost to the floor.

I'm just about to tell Corey to hurry up when I hear people in the hallway. I want to be wrong. I pray I'm wrong, but I know I'm not when I hear the lock turn. His mother is back.

TWELVE

Shoot, it ain't my fault you forgot your phone. Do I look like your secretary?" Corey's mother says. The door opens just a little bit, then stops. "You sure don't pay me like I am."

"I'll find it on my own." It's the guy who was with Corey's mother before. "And watch how you talk to me."

I rush into the bedroom. "Shush," I say, holding my finger to my lips.

I look around for someplace to hide. The only option is behind the bedroom door. The three of them are inside the apartment now. "Boy, where you at?" Corey's mother yells out.

"I'm in the bedroom," Corey answers. He's looking at me through the crack in the door.

"Well, look for Kendal's cell phone while you in there."

Corey doesn't move.

"You see how your boy is just standing there? He ain't looking for nothing. Must be stupid, just like you." Kendal laughs.

I pull my stomach in as he comes into the bedroom.

"Look, it's right there," he says, walking toward the mattress. "Good thing it don't have no teeth or it woulda bit the living daylights out of you."

"No, you can't! I'll get it," Corey says.

"Why? You got somebody in here or something?" Kendal asks, taking another step.

"Who got somebody in here?" Corey's mother says, coming into the bedroom.

"Nobody but me, Mama!" Corey says, throwing himself on his knees after handing Kendal the phone. He wraps his arms around his mother's legs.

"Get off me," she says. "Come on, Kendal, let's go."

Corey stays on his knees until they're gone.

When I step out from my hiding place, my heart is beating like crazy. "That was close."

"Can I still come upstairs with you?" he asks, taking my hand.

"Maybe just for a little while."

Before I know what's happening, Corey leaps up and hugs me, knocking us both against the wall. My sister feelings are trying to work their way up, but I push them back because I'm no longer anybody's sister.

"Hello, children," Miss Shirley says in a cheery voice when we get to my floor. The bells on her cane jingle.

"Hi, Miss Shirley," I say. Corey buries his face in my thigh. "Say hi, Corey."

"Hello, shy one," Miss Shirley says, looking at the welt on his leg.

He peeks out. "Hi," he says, pointing to her cane. "I like your bells and your cape."

Miss Shirley shakes the cane and the bells dance some more. Corey laughs. "And what are you up to this morning?" she asks.

I'm just about to answer when Corey says, "I was afraid, so Dellie said I could go to her house. She's always so nice to me!"

Miss Shirley gives me a good long look, then bends down and places her palm over the welt on Corey's leg. This time he doesn't flinch. It's like she's not even touching it. "Is that right?"

The air between us is filled with words only she and I can hear. *Corey believes in me.*

"Well," Miss Shirley continues as she stands up, "I've got an appointment I need to get to. Enjoy yourselves."

"Dellie, is she a witch?" Corey asks when the elevator door closes.

"Why do you say that?"

"Because only witches wear capes," he says.

"Witches are make-believe and besides, whoever heard of a witch named Miss Shirley?"

"Maybe," Corey says like he's thinking hard, "she's a good witch."

"Nope, no such thing as that either," I say.

When Corey sees the old-fashioned iron we sometimes use as a doorstop when we throw the garbage out, he laughs. "Why you use your iron like that!"

"Shush, not so loud," I say. "We have to be quiet, okay?"

I explain we don't use it to iron clothes.

"My mother got one too. She don't iron clothes with it either. She says I'll just wrinkle them all up anyway."

"Are you hungry?" I ask, not wanting to think about his mother.

Corey's eyes light up. "Yes! Something yummy, please."

The word *supersister* runs through my head and I let it. "Okay, coming right up," I say. "Please, have a seat." I sweep my arm through the air like they do on game shows when someone wins a prize.

"Dellie, do you know my birthday is gonna be here soon?" he asks before sitting.

"Really? How old will you be?"

"I'll be six just like a big boy. Hey," he says, looking around. "Where is everybody?"

"My mother is sleeping and my father is at work."

"You got any sisters or brothers?" he asks.

Too many questions. Panic threatens me. I shake my head.

"Oh. Why you ain't in school?" he asks me.

"'Cause," I say, relieved when the panic goes no further. "I wasn't feeling good this morning and my mother told me to stay home," I lie. "Why aren't you in school?"

"Because my mother didn't feel like taking me. Where your daddy work at?" Corey asks.

"In a factory Down the Back."

"Is he nice, Dellie?"

"Yeah, he is."

"What's it like?" he asks.

I'm searching inside the refrigerator for something Corey can eat. "What's what like?"

He's swinging his legs back and forth. "Having a daddy. What's it like?"

"Um, I guess it's just like having a mother."

"Oh," Corey says.

"Who's this kid?" Corey asks, now standing in front of Louis's picture.

"No," I say when he reaches for the frame on tiptoe. "Don't touch that!"

The sound of my voice makes Corey nervous. He tries to put the frame back, but the rosary beads get in the way and the frame falls to the floor.

I rush over too late. *Oh, no.*

"I'm sorry, I'm sorry. Look, it's okay." Corey sounds scared. He picks up the frame. "It's okay, right?" A small piece of glass has broken off. "It was an accident," he says.

"I know. I didn't mean to scare you. Can I have the frame?"

He holds the frame out and drops of blood fall to the floor.

"Oh my God, you're bleeding. Let me see your hands."

"No, I'm okay." He hides his hands behind his back. "I'm not bleeding."

"Yes, you are. Let me see." I pull his hands out so I can get a good look.

He has two small cuts, one on his index finger and one on his thumb. They sure are bleeding a lot for small cuts. I put Louis's picture back on the shelf and take Corey into the bathroom to pour peroxide over his fingers.

"Ouch!" he yells out.

My mother's bed creaks. "Dellie, is everything okay?" she asks.

Before I can answer, she opens the bathroom door. Her eyebrows are pinched. "What's going on?" she asks, looking from me to Corey.

"Mom, I'm sorry, but he was hungry and then he got cut and then—"

Corey interrupts. "It's all my fault, Miss Dellie's mama. Please don't hit her."

"What? I'm not going to hit anyone." Her face relaxes. "Where are you cut, honey?" When she takes away my nursing duty, I sit on the edge of the bathtub, relieved.

"You're pretty, Miss Dellie's mama," Corey says.

This makes my mother smile. It's a real one too, not one I pretend is real. I see the laugh lines around her eyes. The few brown freckles high on her cheeks reach upward.

"Please, call me Diana. And what's your name?"

My mother dries Corey's fingers, puts a Band-Aid on each one and kisses them.

"Mom, this is Corey. He lives on the first floor."

She nods.

"He has a welt on his leg too. Can you put something on it?"

My mother looks at both legs but doesn't see anything.

"On his calf right here," I say, showing her where. Only it's not there anymore. "Maybe . . ." I think about Miss Shirley touching his leg. "It went away."

"You're a nice mama, Miss Diana," Corey says, distracting me.

"Thank you, sweetheart. Now, what's this about you being hungry? You two can watch television while I make something to eat," my mother says, already heading to the kitchen.

We sit on the couch and Corey snuggles up to me. "You feel nice, Dellie," he says.

"You too." I put my arm around him and point the remote control at the TV. "What do you want to watch?" I ask.

"I don't know."

I change the channels, looking for something funny, but I

can't find anything. The morning cartoons are over and all that's on are soap operas and court shows.

Corey's breathing softly and he feels heavier on me. I lower the TV volume and watch him sleep before closing my own eyes to the sound of my mother humming.

After a while, my mother calls us over to the table.

Corey wakes up and stretches his arms and legs.

"Did you have a good nap?" I ask.

"I wasn't napping, Dellie."

"Yes, you were. I have the drool on my shirt to prove it!"

He hides his laugh behind his hand.

"Seems to me you were both snoring in there," my mother says from the kitchen. "Now, come and eat."

The bottle of pancake syrup is almost empty, so I turn it upside down and put it on the table in front of Corey.

"Why did you put it like that?"

"So you'll get every last drop."

Corey rests his chin on his folded hands. His eyes are on the bottle. "I love pancake syrup. It tastes good on crackers," he says.

"Crackers?" my mother asks, setting his plate on the table. "Well, today you'll have it on waffles. You think you'll like that?"

Corey nods over and over again, then eats like somebody might take the food away before he can finish. "This is gooood," he says before popping another piece of waffle into his mouth.

My mother laughs and gives Corey a kiss on his cheek. It looks to me like Corey is a plant that has just been watered. He sits up straighter and his smile is wider.

"You're the sweetest little boy!" my mother says as she turns the kitchen radio on. I'm surprised the on button still works. It's been a long time since she's listened to the radio.

The radio used to play whenever my mother was in the kitchen. Sometimes, if she really liked the song, she'd turn it up high and shake her hips while chopping onions. It doesn't matter that the music is playing softly now and there's no dancing. My mother isn't cleaning Louis's picture or rocking in the chair watching it, and that's good enough.

When Corey is finished eating, he licks the leftover syrup off the plate. Watching him reminds me of the kind of life he has. The kind where his belly is never full.

My mother washes the dishes while we watch television. After a while, she says she doesn't want Corey's mother to worry about him and that it's time for him to go home.

"I'll take him," I say.

"No," my mother says. "I'll walk him down."

Corey grabs my hand. "Can Dellie take me?"

"I don't know." My mother presses her fingers to her lips.

"Pretty please?" Corey pleads.

"I can do this, Mom. Please, trust me," I whisper.

"Dellie won't let anything bad happen," Corey says.

She looks at me a long time before nodding.

"Don't open the door for anybody, okay?" I say when we're in front of his door.

"I won't, Dellie." Then Corey hugs me.

When he closes his apartment door, Kayla steps into the hallway from outside. She's still mad at me. She hasn't knocked on my door in days.

"Hi," I say, wondering if she's not in school because of the way the kids were acting.

She doesn't say anything back. She takes the steps two at a time.

"Tell me why you're so mad at me, Kayla!" I call to her.

"You know why!"

No, I don't.

"Did you wait for him to go inside?" my mother asks when I get back to my apartment.

"Yeah, I even got a hug."

The music is still playing only it's a little bit louder. "He's such a sweet boy," she says, drumming her fingers against the kitchen table.

"How can his mother be so mean?" I ask.

"I don't know the answer to that," she says, standing. "But I'm very proud of how you watch out for him."

"Really?"

"Yes, really. Now come dance with me."

I think about asking my mother what I should do about Kayla, but I don't want to ruin her good mood.

When my mother spins me, I close my eyes and wonder if Michael likes to dance.

THIRTEEN

My mother's been in a good mood since making Corey breakfast last week, so I ask if I can go out.

She's sitting on the couch reading the Sunday magazine from today's paper. "No," she says. It comes out of her mouth as naturally as her name.

"Why? You trusted me enough to bring Corey downstairs and I was fine."

Her face changes, like she's actually considering letting me go. She starts to say something and for a minute I think she might say yes, but then she shakes her head.

"Dad, please?" I say.

He watches my mother from his chair. "Diana, she's thirteen years old. Let her go."

"No," my mother says. "Nothing can happen to her here, with us."

My father nods yes to me while my mother stares at him in disbelief.

"Thanks, Daddy!" I run to the coat closet. It looks like it might rain, so I grab the first rain jacket I see.

"How can we keep her safe, Alejandro, if she's not with us?" my mother asks.

It sounds like one of those questions people ask not expecting an answer. Only I know my mother really does want somebody to tell her how to keep me safe.

"Diana," my father says, "she's had lots of time to learn how to be safe."

I put on the jacket and wait for my mother to argue some more but she never does. She just cries.

"Mom, I'll be extra careful. Just like when I brought Corey home. I promise."

"I know, I'm just so . . . ," she says through her tears. "Scared."

I've never heard her say that before and it cuts into me. "Don't be, Mom." It's all I can think to say. Then I hug her.

"It'll be okay," Dad says, taking my mother's hand. Then he reaches into his pocket to give me some money.

I kiss them both and leave.

Corey and his mother are outside when I push open the building door. "Hurry up. Just 'cause it's your birthday don't mean I can't whip ya skinny behind. You hear me, boy, or are your ears broke today?" she asks, turning her back to him. Another one of those questions that don't want answers.

When Corey catches my eye, I wink. My father gave me enough money to buy Corey a birthday present. I mouth that he should do what his mother tells him to. He gives me a "humph," then runs to catch up with her. She doesn't say a word to me, but Corey waves as they walk away.

I watch Corey skip beside his mother until I can't see him anymore.

Suddenly Kayla walks past me bumping into me as she goes. "Move out of my way," she says. She looks extra nice today. Her hair is out and she's wearing a headband the same color as her pants.

As if on cue, Alexa strolls past talking junk. "You should stop spending what little money you have on matching outfits. You should buy some food instead."

Kayla walks faster. Her hands tighten into fists at her sides.

"Wait up," I call out to her ignoring Alexa.

She stops but doesn't turn around. "What do you want?"

"I want us to be friends again, but first you have to tell me why you're so mad at me."

"You told everybody how my mother had to sell our stuff like we were some kind of desperate beggars," she says, facing me. "Now everybody knows just how poor I am, *that's* why!"

"I did not! And who cares anyway? Everybody here is poor!"

"Don't you get it? *I* care. I don't even belong here."

"*Belong* here? What does that even mean, Kayla?"

"I just know it was you," she says.

"Tell me, since you seem to know everything, why would I do that?"

"How should I know? Maybe you're jealous of me or something," she says.

"You know I'm not like that."

Just then Bryan walks into the courtyard. I've never seen him around here before. "Oh, yeah?" Kayla says. Her light eyes narrow and don't look so pretty now. "Remember when you wished you had my clothes because they were better than yours?"

I do, but I don't tell her.

We stare at each other without saying another thing. Bryan laughs.

Miss Shirley walks toward us. She's not wearing her cape today. I guess it's too warm for it. She's wearing a long black skirt with pink flowers, silver sandals, a green and white striped shirt, and a pink sweater. Instead of a turban, she's wearing a baseball cap. Even though her clothes are mismatched, I think she looks pretty.

"Hello, ladies," Miss Shirley says when she reaches us. "Is there some*ting* I can help you two with? You both look madder than a wet cat."

Kayla crosses her arms. "No, thank you."

"I told you. It wasn't me!" I say.

"Now, girls," Miss Shirley interupts. "It's not right for two friends to be yelling at each other, especially young ladies like yourselves."

Kayla's voice is trembling like she wants to cry. "It had to be you, Dellie! You're the only one I told."

"You're crazy! I promised you I wouldn't say anything and I didn't!"

"I'm crazy? I'm not the one who pushed my brother into the street so he could get killed!" she snaps back, and then covers her mouth.

The world stops and the panic has returned. There isn't any air to breathe and everything seems far away. Tears fill my eyes and I can't stop them.

"Kayla!" Miss Shirley says, tapping her cane on the ground three times. "I just know you don't mean that."

Kayla doesn't look away from the cane. "No, I didn't . . . ," she whispers.

Miss Shirley nods like she already knew the answer. "It is good to get *tings* out of your system," she says to me, wiping my wet face with a tissue. "Tears help to carry bad *tings* out. If you don't let them come, they will stay inside, watering your bad feelings until they are wild and ugly weeds."

It doesn't feel good to be crying outside where everybody can see me. People sitting on the benches are staring at us.

"I'm okay," I say, pushing Miss Shirley's tissue from my face. "I have to go now." I storm off, not caring which direction I go.

Tears stream down my face and I can't think clearly. I search the sky. *Louis, I'm so sorry.*

After a while, I find myself in front of the community center. Alexa is standing outside the doors with Michael. For a second, seeing him takes my breath away. And when Alexa says something into his ear, I wonder if she's won, and I get a bad feeling. I press it in with the rest of my bad feelings, except this one sits on top like it doesn't fit.

Michael calls me over, but I just can't make myself go. Besides, Alexa will be gloating and I can't take a chance of losing it again, not in front of Michael. If he wants to hang out with her instead of me, let him. We've only shared an umbrella and a few words that didn't really mean anything anyway.

FOURTEEN

Enjoying my freedom, I go the long way through the playground to a store where I can buy Corey a birthday gift. When I get to the swings, I sit on one, thinking about Kayla and the mean things she said to me. I should've done something, anything other than cry and run away.

After a while, Kayla and Bryan walk into the playground and watch some boys playing basketball not too far from me.

Bryan lights a cigarette, then tucks another behind his ear.

"Can I have a little of that?" Kayla asks, reaching for his lit cigarette.

A tangled breath gets stuck in her throat and becomes a wild coughing fit. She jumps around and fans her face. As far as I know, she's never smoked before. She's just doing it now to look cool for Bryan, I guess. But she doesn't look cool, she looks stupid.

When Bryan laughs, it sounds like he's the one who's choking. Thinking this makes me laugh too.

"What're you laughing at?" Bryan asks.

I ignore his bad attitude and get up from the swing. I still can't figure out why Kayla would like somebody like that.

"Nice raincoat," he says. "Isn't it kind of, um, I don't know . . . gigantic?"

I look down at my rain jacket, except it's not my jacket. I put my mother's on by mistake. Bryan's right, it is gigantic on me. The only good thing is the pockets are nice and big. Big enough to hide my balled-up hands.

"Later, Bry," Kayla says.

"Aw, come on, Kayla. Don't go. Hang with me."

Kayla giggles, then Bryan kisses her. I can't imagine kissing anybody but Michael. His lips look soft and pillowy, nothing at all like Bryan's chapped ones.

I want to get as far away from Kayla as possible. When I start to walk away, Bryan yells, "Hey, you know you want some of this. Maybe next time it'll be your turn!"

I'm staring at him and whatever I say has to be good. "Newsflash! I would never kiss a boy who's been left back as many times as you!" I shout as loud as I can.

"Oh, snap, Bryan," one of the guys watching the game says. "She burned you legit!"

Some of the other guys start laughing and that makes Bryan madder than ever. He glares and suddenly I wish I'd kept my mouth closed. "Man, shut up!" he says, punching his fist into his palm.

I start to run, putting as much distance as I can between me and Bryan, and that's good—except the boys are still laughing and I know *that* can't be good.

FIFTEEN

The store is crowded today. The registers aren't working, so everything is being added up by hand. Some customers lose their patience and put exact change on the counter before walking out.

I look around, but I don't know what to get Corey. I have no idea what a six-year-old boy will like. Louis didn't make it to six.

There are a bunch of toys on a spinning rack by the newspapers. One is a soldier with painted eyes too big for his face. There's also a small race car, a box of alphabet flash cards with fish on them, jacks, a miniature game of checkers and a whoopee cushion. Deciding won't be easy.

Making a set of flash cards out of cardboard is simple, so they're out. Now, the whoopee cushion is something a kid will like no matter how old they are, and since teaching Corey to play checkers will be fun, he'll get two presents instead of one.

I turn down an aisle, trying to find chocolate cupcakes, and bump right into Kayla and Bryan. "Watch where you're going," Bryan says, towering over me.

"Why're you following me?" I ask, backing into the shelves.

"We're not." Bryan holds up a bag of potato chips to my face. "What, you think you're the only one who needs stuff from the store?"

It seems like Kayla is about to say something to me, but she stops short. "Come on, let's just go, Bryan."

"Dellie," someone calls while I'm in line. "Why didn't you come over when I called you? Didn't you hear me?"

It's Michael. My stomach rises and then falls when I think of him standing with Alexa. "Yeah, I did, but I was in a rush."

"Oh," he says, taking a step closer. "Well, I, um . . . wanted to ask you something."

"Really?"

He nods. "I was wondering if we could hang out sometime." His arm touches mine and I don't want him to move away. It feels like there's some sort of invisible thread connecting us now.

"Where's Alexa?" I ask, catching my reflection in the frozen-food case to check on my hair, but I can't get a good enough look.

"I don't know." He shrugs. "We were supposed to be

tutoring, but nobody showed up. I'm glad, though, now that I've run into you."

This is really happening. The boy I like likes me back. "Oh," I say, hoping harder than ever my mother won't ruin this for me.

Michael returns my smile and suddenly I'm thinking about kissing him and whether or not his lips are as soft as they look.

"Can I have your number?" he asks, whipping out a pen and a small piece of paper.

In the neatest handwriting possible, I write it down for him.

"Sweet," he says when I give the pen and paper back. "I'll call you." He walks out of the store backward, still smiling.

As soon as he's out of sight, I take a deep breath and close my eyes. I'm trying to keep cool, but what I really want is to laugh out loud or dance or just anything.

"Move up," someone says, pushing into me.

"Can you give me some room?" I turn and find myself face-to-face with Bryan again. He's so close I smell his cigarette breath.

"Be quiet," he says, breaking out into a weird crooked smile. "Nobody wants to be close to you."

I look for Kayla but she's nowhere around.

The line starts to move and Bryan bumps into me again. "What're you doing? Back off, you're too close,"

I say, trying not to sound as scared as I suddenly feel.

"I'm not close to you," he says. "Move up."

Finally, I pay for my stuff and the clerk hands me my bag.

"Why don't you put your stuff in those giant pockets instead of that geeky bag?" Bryan asks.

"Maybe because I don't want to. Why do you care where I put it anyway?"

Bryan grabs at my jacket pocket. "See, you have plenty of room," he says, squeezing the outside of it. "Oh, you already have stuff in there!" His voice is loud.

"What? No, I don't."

Kayla walks over to Bryan, holding a bottle of soda. "What did you do?" she whispers to him.

The clerk is staring at us now.

I stick my hand into my pocket and pull out a big pack of bubble gum that doesn't belong to me. I hold the pocket open and see three packs of mints, a small bottle of hand sanitizer, a shiny nail clipper on a chain and a candy bar. "What is all this? This stuff isn't mine."

Before I'm able to stop him, Bryan jams his hand into my pocket and pulls everything out. Some of it falls on the floor. Kayla bends down to pick it up, but Bryan stops her. "I'll do it," he says.

He picks it all up and dramatically places each piece on the counter next to the cash register while I stand gaping.

Everyone is staring. The clerk shakes his head like he's trying to stop a fly from landing on it. He says something in Arabic and it doesn't sound good at all.

When a man in the back of the line asks what the holdup is, a lady calls out, "Somebody was caught stealing!"

My heart beats in my throat. The register guy yells something at me, but I don't know what he's saying. His face twists up, and when I don't answer him, he repeats it and this time it's in English. "You are stealer, you are stealer!"

"No! No, I'm not! I don't know how those things got into my pocket!" My voice doesn't sound like it's mine.

"You pay for all this now!" the clerk says, banging his hand on the counter.

"No, I don't want any of it!" I try to think of something else to say to make him believe me. "I-I don't even like this kind of gum!"

"You better come up with something better than that," the lady says.

When Bryan yells, "Call 911. She's a thief!" Everything falls into place and I feel stupid for not thinking of it earlier. All that bumping into me. He put those things in my pocket and now he wants the police to come. He's gone way too far.

"No! He did it," I say, pointing to Bryan.

Kayla's staring at Bryan like she knows he did it too, but she doesn't say a word.

"Who's burned now?" he whispers to me. When he turns

to the long line of customers, his smile is big and dumb. "I caught a thief!" he says proudly.

"I can't believe you're doing this," I say, pushing the tears from my cheeks.

One person claps. Not an enthusiastic clap but one that sounds like it's missing some claps in between. "Whatever. Now can you both move so that somebody else can pay for their stuff?"

"Just get out," the register guy says to me. "Just go! You are not ever allowed back into store. You are a no-good thief. A stealer, stealer."

"But he did it," I say.

"Do your ears work?" the register guy screams. "Get out of store!"

Finally I run out, turning once to make sure the register guy isn't following me. He's not, but he's got his angry face pressed up against the door, in between advertisements for cold beer and an egg sale—making sure I don't sneak back inside.

I walk home in the rain, so glad Michael wasn't there for that mess.

SIXTEEN

My mother jumps off the couch the second I walk through the door. "Are you all right? You were gone for so long. Where were you?" she asks, pushing my wet hair from my face. "And why are you wearing my raincoat?"

If she finds out about the store thing, she might never trust me again. "I'm fine. I just went for a walk," I say, forcing a smile and undoing the buttons on the jacket. "I put it on by mistake."

"I told you she'd be okay," my father says from the kitchen table, where he's doing a crossword puzzle.

My mother looks away and nods.

I kiss her cheek, knowing her mind must've been going a mile a minute thinking about the things that could've happened.

When the phone rings, I'm afraid it's someone calling to tell my mom about the store. I try to disappear into my room as she listens to the voice on the other end, but it's too late.

I can't read her face at all when she calls me using my full name.

"Carmen heard there was some excitement at the store just now. Do you know anything about it?" Mom taps her top lip with her finger. She does this when she's waiting for a lie.

I want to throw up. "Who's Carmen?" I ask, trying to buy some time.

"Carmen, from my job," my mother says, resting her hands on her hips.

"Oh, right," I say. "That Carmen."

My father goes to my mother's side. "Is there something you should be telling us, Dellie?" he asks.

The one time she lets me out, something bad happens. I'm so mad at Bryan, I could scream. He's ruined everything. "Well . . . ," I start.

My mother begins to pace. "I can't believe this." She looks to my father, then back to me. "I knew it was a bad idea. Why did you take those things, Delilah, huh? Have we raised you to be a thief?" I watch her earrings swing back and forth.

"You stole?" my father asks disgustedly.

"No, Dad! I didn't take anything. A boy from school put those things in my pocket, I swear . . ." My voice cracks between *didn't* and *take*. I should've known somebody was bound to recognize me. I think about everything that's happened today and all I want is for my mother to hug me and say that it'll all be okay. "Mom . . ."

She puts her hand up like she's stopping traffic. The lines on her palm are much darker than the rest of her hand. "Please, if you're about to swear on a lie, stop right there and get your jacket on. We're going down to the store."

"What? *No!*"

"You have to apologize." She slips the strap of her pocketbook over her shoulder.

"But Dad," I say, hoping he'll stop this. "They said I can never go into the store again."

"You should've thought about that before you put those things into your pocket," he answers.

"I already told you I didn't. It was Bryan, Kayla's stupid boyfriend. He kept bumping into me and put all that stuff into my pocket."

"Kayla?" my mother asks.

I nod hopefully.

"So Kayla knows it wasn't you?"

"Yes."

"Since when does Kayla have a boyfriend?" my mother asks.

"I don't know! We're not friends anymore, haven't you noticed?"

"Hey," my father says, startling me. "Watch your attitude."

"Sorry."

"Tell me again. What happened?" my mother says.

"She thinks I said some stuff about her," I say, plopping down on a kitchen chair.

"Did you, Dellie?"

"No, Mom. Don't you know I wouldn't do anything like that?"

My mother watches me for a few seconds before saying, "Of course I know. Let's go."

Not again. "Where?"

"To Kayla's. I want to see if she'll go back to the store with us to clear up this whole mess."

"I'm coming too," my father says, stepping toward the doorway.

"No." My mother walks past him and opens the door. "I can handle this," she says.

"Are you sure?" he asks, surprised.

"Very."

In the hallway, Miss Shirley is unlocking her apartment door. There's a grocery bag on the floor by her feet. "Hello," she says to my mother. "I'm Shirley." She smiles at me. "I moved in a few weeks ago."

"Hi, I'm Diana. It's nice to meet you," Mom says, shaking Miss Shirley's hand. "And this is my husband, Alejandro."

My father waves.

"And this is our daughter, Dellie."

"Oh, yes, I've already met Dellie. She's a sweet girl

and you are blessed." Miss Shirley smiles at me again.

I nod, embarrassed.

My mother smiles her thanks and reaches for Miss Shirley's bag. "Let me get that for you."

I suddenly feel guilty about Miss Shirley having to go to the store herself.

"Wonderful," Miss Shirley pushes her door open. "Please, come in. I was planning on making some tea and I'd love to have company to share it with."

"That sounds very nice," my mother says. "But we're on our way out."

"Maybe another time then. Before you go, though, may I ask you a favor?"

"Sure, what is it?" my mother asks.

"I was wondering if Dellie could run a few errands for me a couple of times a week." Miss Shirley rubs her lower back. "On the days I'm not feeling up to it."

I snap to attention. If my mother agrees, I won't have to beg to be let out anymore.

"Well," my mother says, like she's seriously thinking about it, "I don't like her wandering around alone."

"There'll be no wandering. Just the errand and back, right, Dellie?" Miss Shirley asks.

"Right."

The air feels awkward now, like there's something heavy hanging over us.

Miss Shirley places her hand on my mother's arm. "No need to worry, dear." Her voice is soothing and for a second, nothing else in the world matters except the sound of it. "She's a big girl. How else will she flourish if you don't put your trust in her?"

It could be my imagination, but I think I see my mother's shoulders relax. "You're right," she says. "But just to the store and back."

Then the air is normal again. "Okay, Mom." I can feel the smile spreading across my face.

"Fantastic," Miss Shirley says. "That'll do an old woman just fine." I wonder if she knows it does me fine too.

"Visit anytime, you hear?" she says.

"We will," my mother answers. "Thank you."

Going up to Kayla's apartment with my mother makes me feel like I'm a little kid. Kayla's mother is not exactly the believing type anyway. I learned that a few months ago.

Kayla was missing her English homework, and Mr. Merrick, our teacher, wrote a note home to Kayla's mother. It was just a note to let her know Kayla needed to make the homework up. No biggie. So, when Kayla's mother showed up during class demanding that Mr. Merrick go searching through his desk for Kayla's misplaced homework, the whole class was shocked.

Kayla put her head down on her desk, trying to hide.

Mr. Merrick, who is always soft-spoken and polite, peered over his glasses and offered to go through his desk later on in the day or even after school, but she wouldn't agree to it. Kayla's mother stood there tapping her toes like she was counting the seconds.

Finally, after fifteen minutes, Mr. Merrick lost his patience. He slammed the book he was holding down on his desk and asked the class monitor to get the assistant principal. That was the only way to get Kayla's mother off his back and out of his classroom. After she left, Mr. Merrick apologized to the class and let us have free time.

At lunch, Kayla told me she lied about the homework but never thought her mother would come to school and try to clear things up herself.

My mother knocks on Kayla's door using the door knocker. Bink, bink, bink. We wait. Bink, bink, bink. No answer. Then my mother puts her ear to the door and uses her knuckles to knock. Thunk, thunk, thunk. Three times again. This time, we hear the peephole lid moving. My mother looks straight into the tiny round window.

The lock turns and the door finally opens and we're hit with the smell of something cooking, but it's not a good smell. At least, it doesn't smell like something I'd want to eat.

Kayla's mother is wearing an apron. Her mouth is smiling but her eyes aren't. Her hair is up in a neat bun and she's wearing a string of huge pearls. Kayla is lounging on the couch behind her but joins her mother in the doorway when she sees it's us.

"Hello, ladies," Kayla's mother says.

"Hi," my mother returns. "I'm sorry to bother you, Christine, but it seems that Kayla's boyfriend has gotten my daughter into trouble down at the store and now she's not allowed to shop there anymore."

Kayla's mother puts her arm around Kayla's shoulders.

"What? You must be thinking about somebody else. My daughter isn't allowed to have a boyfriend yet." She looks at me. "Dellie, you must be mistaken."

"I don't think so." My mother's voice has the tiniest laugh in it. "Maybe the boy isn't her boyfriend." She looks over at Kayla. "Let's just say he's her friend."

"I've raised my Kayla to stand for what's right. If she saw something, she would've spoken up." She pinches Kayla's shoulder good and long. "Isn't that a fact?"

Kayla flinches a little. "I don't know what you're talking about, Dellie." Her voice is a whisper. "I don't have a boyfriend and I wasn't at the store today. If you got into trouble, it's your fault." She glances nervously at her mother, who pats her shoulder.

"Now that you've heard the truth," Kayla's mother says, "I suggest you and Dellie leave."

My mother puts her hand up to the door frame. She isn't

about to let this go. "Look, this is getting out of control. I don't think you completely understand." Her voice echoes through the hallway. "Kayla's *friend* did something that is wrong. She must've seen the whole thing. All she has to do is tell the guys at the store what she knows. That's it."

Kayla's mother speaks through her teeth. "I'm sorry, Diana. Your daughter doesn't know what she's talking about." She looks directly at me. The skin under her right eye is jumping. "Didn't you hear when Kayla said she wasn't at the store?"

With that, she slams the door in our faces. My mother grunts, then reaches for the doorknob. "Mom, no!" I whisper. "We just can't go walking into somebody's house."

She seems to hear me and takes her hand off the knob. "I'm so sorry you had to see this, Dellie," she says as we walk down the steps. "I should've never dragged you up here in the first place."

Corey is sitting at the kitchen table when we get back. My mother smiles big and her voice gets singsongy the minute she sees him. She doesn't look or sound like somebody who just got a door slammed in her face. "Hi, honey."

"Hi, Miss Dellie's mama," Corey says shyly. "Do you know it's my birthday?"

"It is?" My mother gives him a birthday kiss. "Then happy birthday!"

"That means we'll have to sing to you," my father says.

He opens a four pack of cupcakes and sticks a candle in one of them.

"I'll get your presents," I say.

When Corey sits on the whoopee cushion, his eyes pop wide open. "Oh, no!" He fans his face. "Stinky."

He laughs so hard his face turns red and he doubles over.

"I think you've been eating too many beans," my mother says.

"Happy birthday, fart boy!" I laugh.

We play two games of checkers, then it's time for another cupcake. When Corey makes his birthday wish, he closes his eyes and smiles a sweet closed-mouth smile. I see a dimple high in his cheek for the first time and I wonder what he wishes for.

Just before I bring Corey downstairs, he says to my mother, "I like you."

"I like you too." Her voice is soft.

And just like that, Bryan and the trouble he caused disappear.

SEVENTEEN

Hey everybody," Shayna says when I walk into math class. "Guard your stuff or it'll get jacked."

I look at Kayla, hurt. I bet she couldn't wait to tell everyone the wrong version of what happened at the store.

"Hey Dellie," Rihanna says. "Sephora has really nice makeup. You think you can get me some with your *special* discount?"

"I didn't steal anything!" I say, taking my seat.

Rihanna looks straight at Kayla. "Oh, I get it. You only do that for your poor friends, right?"

From the way everybody laughs, you'd think Chris Rock just walked in cracking jokes. Kayla doesn't pick up her head. She busies herself with cleaning out her backpack, but I can see the tears starting.

As the rest of the kids come in, Shayna makes it her business to let each of them know I'm a thief.

"What's up, Dellie?" Michael says, standing in front of my desk.

"Didn't you hear what Shayna said?" Alexa cuts in, like she's got top-secret information. "Dellie's a klepto." She laughs.

"No, I'm not!" There's a chance he'll believe her since he did see me in the store yesterday.

"Stop lying, Dellie!" Alexa says.

Kayla gives Alexa a dirty look and I think maybe this time she'll do something, but then Mr. Dumbrewski stomps into class. "Why," he says, "is it so noisy in here?"

Michael rushes to his seat. Alexa starts to fill Mr. Dumbrewski in about me stealing, but he stops her before she can finish. "Seems like," he says, "you're spreading an ugly rumor about a classmate." Everyone is quiet. "Maybe this is something the principal should be aware of. Would you like to go to his office and fill him in?"

Xavier snorts. "That's what you get," he says to Alexa quietly.

Alexa's face goes all smooth with embarrassment. "No."

"Good!" Mr. Dumbrewski says. "Let's get to work, people. Finals are just around the corner."

I have a hard time paying attention to the math lesson. All I'm able to think about is Kayla's betrayal and whether Michael thinks I'm a thief.

The rest of the school day is a blur and when it's over, I'm the first one out the door.

When I get to our courtyard, I look for Corey, but he's nowhere in sight. In the building, there's no sound coming from his apartment, but all of a sudden, loud talking fills the hallway.

"The next time I tell you to do something, you better hop to it quick, you hear me?"

Corey's mother is dragging him by the wrist, but he's pulling back. "You're hurting me, Mommy!" His face is soaked in tears.

She slaps him and his head twists to the side. "Now, that's something to cry over. You want more, huh?" she asks, raising her hand again.

Fear takes hold of my feet the same way it did when Louis was hit by the car, but I fight it. "No! Leave him alone," I scream, stepping closer.

"Dellie!" Corey cries.

"He is none of your business," his mother says, flinging Corey to the floor like a piece of junk. He lands by his door and while she searches her pockets for her keys, I run to him, but she blocks me. "He's not your brother or something! He's my son, you hear me? Mine."

Panic takes hold of my heart, sending the quiet terror to every part of me. "Corey!"

He gets to his knees and tries to grab hold of my hand. I'm desperate to get him away from her.

"Are you crazy, boy?" she says, hitting his back.

My breathing is out of control. "No!" I howl, like it's me she's hitting.

"Have you lost your mind?" Mrs. Lawrence is unexpectedly standing by my side. "Don't you touch him again!" she says.

"I'll do what I want," Corey's mother answers.

"I'm calling the police," Mrs. Lawrence says. "Come with me, Dellie."

"I'm not leaving him!"

Mrs. Lawrence hesitates before hurrying up the steps as fast as she can, thanks to the elevator being broken again. "Do not go near her, Dellie!"

Corey's mother yanks him up by the back of his shirt before unlocking the door. I'm only able to take his hand for a second before she pushes him into the apartment and slams the door.

Something inside falls. "Get back here!" Corey's mother says.

"Leave him alone!" I turn the doorknob but it's locked.

"No," Corey wails. "I promise to be good next time!"

A loud smack, then, "There is no next time 'cause I'm going to teach you a lesson right now."

"Corey! Corey!" I pound on the door using both hands.

"Dellie!" It sounds muffled, like maybe there's something over his face.

"Leave him alone!" Now I start kicking the door.

Corey's mother laughs. "That little girl can't help you!"

Another slapping noise, more falling things. "Ow, Mommy, no!"

Corey's crying drops me to my knees. "Stop it, stop it!" My throat is raw. "What are you doing to him?"

Other people crowd into the hallway now. Miss Shirley is standing behind me. "Dellie," she says in a rushed voice. "What is happening?"

"I saw her beating Corey!" I reach up to the doorknob. "I have to help him."

Mrs. Lawrence is back. "The police are on the way," she says.

"It'll be okay," Miss Shirley says, trying to pull me to my feet. "The police station is only around the corner. Let's go."

"No. I can't leave until I know he's all right." I start, turning the knob wildly. "Corey!"

Three policemen take their time entering the hallway. They must have already been patrolling our blocks. "What's the trouble here?" one asks.

Mrs. Lawrence starts to fill them in.

"Dellie, the police are here now. Let them take care of it," Miss Shirley says. "There's nothing more you can do."

My hands slip from the door.

"That's right," Miss Shirley says, helping me to my feet. "Let's get you upstairs now, and later you can come on over for some tea. It'll help to calm you."

Tea isn't going to make me feel better. Nothing will.

My mother's face drops when she sees me and Miss Shirley standing at the door. My parents are never home this early. "What is it, Dellie? What's happened?" my mother asks, shutting the radio off.

My father takes me in his arms. "Are you hurt, mami?"

"She's okay," Miss Shirley says. "But she has witnessed Corey's mother beating him, and from what I gather, she was very brave and tried to stop it from happening."

"Oh, no!" my mother says, pulling me to her.

"The police are here now. More than likely they're going to take that boy away," Miss Shirley says.

I break away from my mother and run to the window. An ambulance is parked beside one of the police cars. A policeman and one of the EMTs walk out of our building. Corey is between them. All three get into the ambulance. My heart hurts.

"I'll be getting home now," Miss Shirley whispers. "I've invited Dellie over for some tea when she's up for it, if that's all right with you."

My mother nods, then closes the door behind her.

"How could Corey's mother hurt him . . ." I almost don't want to finish thinking about how I hurt Louis. "On purpose," I add.

"Mami," my father says, rubbing my back. "Some people in this world are crazy. It's like their brains don't connect the way they should. We'll pray for Corey and hope things will change for him."

My mother kisses my forehead. I bury my face in her neck and cry.

"Dellie, baby, Dellie, baby," she says. "It's okay, he'll be fine."

She never spoke those words for Louis, so I dare to believe her.

In Miss Shirley's apartment, music plays. It sounds like the end of a movie I had to watch once in science class.

Miss Shirley pours steaming hot water into two mugs. "Is that peppermint tea?" I sniff the air.

"Yes, it is. It's good for sending bad feelings on their way." She smiles, then adds, "I like a bit of honey in mine. Would you like some too?"

I nod.

Miss Shirley squeezes honey onto a small spoon and dunks it into our mugs. "Perfect," she says, taking a sip.

I take a sip too; it's sweet and good.

"How could Corey's mother be so mean to him? I thought parents are always supposed to love their kids." My eyes still burn from the crying I did.

"Yes, but sometimes people either don't do what they're supposed to do, or they simply don't know how," she answers.

Even after I hurt Louis and made my parents' lives hard and painful, it seems like they still love me. "How do you know the difference between when someone is doing what they're supposed to be doing and when they really love you?"

Miss Shirley puts her tea down and studies my face. "Love is strong. It can hold on, no matter how much it gets tugged or stretched. I don't think you need to concern yourself with the difference, Dellie."

I think she's wrong. "But can it be strong enough for me even when I'm . . . the reason my little brother, Louis, is dead?"

"Tell me, Dellie." Miss Shirley's voice is as smooth as the honey. "What happened, child?"

The words I've been holding in for so long tumble out. "Last year, I was playing with Louis outside. He was on his bike and I was pushing him from behind because he couldn't pedal very fast." The knot in my throat tightens. "He said he wanted to go faster than the wind." I smile, thinking about how he looked to the sky when he said *wind.* "I ran faster than ever and before I knew what was happening, we were in the middle of Bellmore Avenue. A horn blew and then there was a long screech. I didn't know where it was coming from but it was loud, much louder than our laughter. And then"—I pause—"I was standing by myself and my brother was lying in the street. I couldn't move. I wanted to be dead, Miss Shirley."

"This is too heavy a weight for you to carry." Miss Shirley takes my hand and gently rubs it. "You did not mean to run into the street," she says. "You did not mean for your brother to get hurt."

My voice strains inside my throat. "But I should have stopped in time. I should have been running slower to begin with."

"You would have done those *tings* if you had known what was going to happen."

Her eyes are soft and kind.

"Miss Shirley, is love strong enough for me even after what I've done?"

Her smile gets wide. "That's when it's the strongest." She tightens her hands around mine. "You can believe it, Dellie."

My hand is sore from banging on Corey's door.

"Do you think Corey's mother just doesn't know how to be a parent?"

"Perhaps not, but that doesn't mean she can't learn. Everybody can learn."

I don't know who'll teach her, but I hope they hurry up.

EIGHTEEN

It's a half day at school, so I'm home early. The closer we get to the end of school, the more of them we'll have. Too bad there's nothing for me to do but read, watch television and look out the window. I hate to admit it, but I miss Kayla. If she wasn't being so hardheaded, we could be bored together. Instead I'm stuck at my window listening to people talk on the benches.

"I saw when that poor boy was put into the ambulance. A terrible sight," Mr. Brown says.

"I heard his mother gets beat herself by her mean-looking boyfriend," Miss Liz says. "You have to feel a little sad for her too in a way."

"Yeah, that may be true and all, but even a dog don't hurt her puppies." That's Miss Etta speaking. "She's a grown woman who should know better, beat or not."

I don't know how I should feel. Part of me wants Corey to stay away forever. If he's away from his mother, she can't hurt him anymore. The other part of me wants him back even if it means he'll be in that apartment. At least he'll be with me again. But that's selfish.

Miss Shirley is coming toward the building. All conversation stops cold when she gets closer. Mr. Brown tips his hat.

"Hey Shirley, how are you today?" Mrs. Lawrence asks.

"I'm just fine. How can I not be on such a beautiful spring day?"

"It's sure nice at the moment, but they're calling for rain," Mrs. Lawrence returns.

"No matter. A good soaking will do the flowers good." Miss Shirley takes a deep breath. "This is my favorite time of the year."

When Miss Shirley's gone, Miss Liz shakes her head. "Have you seen that woman in her cape?"

Miss Etta laughs. "Maybe she's some sort of witch."

"She just likes her cape. You-all should give her a chance. She's a very nice woman. Makes a good cup of tea too," Mrs. Lawrence says.

After a little bit, the sky clouds over and it starts to rain. The courtyard clears out fast.

When the phone rings, I pick it up before it has a chance to ring twice. "Hello?"

"Hello. Could I—I mean, this is Michael. May I speak to Dellie?"

"Hi, it's Dellie." I grin into the phone.

"Are you busy?"

Trying to sound cool, like I get calls from boys all the time, I say, "No, just watching television." Kayla would be proud of me.

"I'm going bowling with some friends. I was wondering if you wanted to come?"

I want to say yes more than anything, but I know I can't. "My parents are at work."

"Oh." He's quiet for a second and then, "Are you avoiding me for some reason?"

The truth is, for the past two weeks, I've been avoiding everybody. If I keep a low profile long enough, they'll forget about the klepto thing and leave me alone. So far, it's working.

"No," I lie.

"I don't believe what they said about you stealing."

"Thanks," I squeak out, relieved.

The line goes quiet and I'm starting to wonder if he heard me, but then he says, "Do you . . ."

When he doesn't finish, I ask, "Do I what?"

"Never mind," he says, sounding like he's in a rush all of a sudden. "I'll see you in school."

I wonder what he was going to ask.

My window is open just a crack so I can smell the rain, cool off the warm cement. Fat raindrops give a little bounce when they hit the ground. The wind is blowing the grass back and forth and when I sniff in deep, I smell the wet dirt too.

Alexa comes out of her building, popping open her umbrella. My stomach feels queasy as I think maybe she's going bowling too.

I keep my eyes on her for as long as possible, but then I spot Corey walking toward the courtyard with a woman I've never seen before.

The woman has short, curly hair and is wearing a flowery dress and a white sweater. She's smiling at Corey as he tries to jump over the puddles.

Walking behind Corey and the woman is Corey's mother. She's carrying a small duffel bag over her shoulder.

I grab the mailbox key and rush out of my apartment and down the steps to the first floor. The mailboxes are on the wall opposite Corey's apartment door.

I put the tiny mailbox key into the lock just as Corey and the two women walk into the hallway and the elevator door opens. Miss Shirley steps out of the elevator and joins me at the mailboxes.

"Hey Dellie!" Corey yells out. There's a scratch on his face and his left arm is in a sling. His fingers stick out of a cast.

Corey tries to hug me with one arm. I don't know how to react in front of his mother, so instead of hugging him back, I just stand there.

Miss Shirley smiles. "Love sure is strong," she says.

Her words turn something on inside of me.

"Hi, Corey," I say finally.

The woman with Corey is very pretty. She's wearing pearl earrings that match her necklace. A few freckles dot her light brown face and I like her right away when she smiles so kindly at Corey. "So this is the famous Dellie," she says.

"Yes, Miss Sandra," Corey says, sneaking a worried look at his mother. She doesn't notice, though. She's searching her pockets for her house keys.

"She's as pretty as you said," Miss Sandra beams.

Corey lets out a giggle, which gets his mother's attention. Her face is scrunched up like she smells something bad. She squints at me and pushes her lips out. "Oh, how you doin'?" she says.

Her hair is pulled back into a tiny ponytail with a fat rubber band. Her skin is ashy gray and looks like she needs to give it a drink. She looks mean and I freeze up.

Miss Shirley winks at me and starts looking through her mail. "I-I'm okay," I stammer.

"I'm Sandra Cumberland, a friend of Corey's family." She holds her hand out.

"Nice to meet you, Miss Cumberland," I take her hand. Her skin is soft.

"Please, call me Miss Sandra."

She gives me her card. Her name and two phone numbers are printed on it along with *Certified Social Worker*. She's more than just a friend. She's here to help Corey.

Corey's mother finally unlocks their door. She slides the duffel bag into the apartment with her wet shoe and goes inside.

"Time to show me your room, sweetheart," Miss Sandra says, holding her hand out to Corey.

"Wait." I'm not ready for him to leave yet. "I'm glad you're back, Corey." I get down on one knee and kiss his cheek. "And I'm glad you're safe," I whisper.

"Me too," he says, shaking his head slowly. "That was a very bad day, Dellie."

I study his face before looking down at my hands, remembering my panic and how hard I tried to help him. It was the second-worst day of my life.

He brightens a little. "But everything's fine now. You don't have to worry anymore."

I hope he's right. "Okay."

Corey's mother appears in the doorway. Her frown is longer now. I don't think she knows how to do anything else. "Boy, come on inside," she says. "Miss Cumberland don't have all day, ya know."

At the sound of his mother's voice, Corey grows silent. Miss Shirley starts to make her way back toward the elevator. Her bells echo off the walls. When she pauses at Corey's open apartment door, we hear Corey's mother fall to the floor. "Stupid wet shoes," she says.

She must be throwing her shoes against the wall. One

thump and then two. If Miss Shirley was a witch, I'd think she just put a spell on Corey's mother.

"Ready, Corey?" Miss Sandra asks.

"See you later, Dellie," he says.

"Miss Shirley," I call when the door closes behind them.

"Yes?"

"You think she'll learn today?" I ask as the elevator door opens.

"Could be, Dellie. We'll just have to watch out for him."

"I'll watch out for him like crazy."

"It would be impossible for you to do any*ting* else. Your heart wouldn't allow it."

One hard look at the bullet hole and I know she's right.

NINETEEN

A week later, Corey is just coming out of his apartment when I go down to get the mail. He's having a hard time holding on to a basketball because of his cast, so I rush to help him.

"Thanks, Dellie," he says.

"You're welcome. Want to come upstairs with me?"

Since coming home, he's been busy playing with kids his age, so I'll be happy to have him to myself.

"Can't, I'm going to play with my friends."

I'm disappointed and happy for him all at the same time. "Are you sure?" I ask, peeking into his apartment.

"Uh-huh," he says.

When I see Corey's mother stirring something in a pot on the stove, I'm shocked. The beat-up chair is covered with a sheet tucked in on the sides and the only thing on the small table is the television that used to be on the floor. "Corey," she says, coming to the door, "I thought you were hungry.

I'm making you some mac and cheese. Come back inside."

Corey rolls his eyes. "But I wanted to go out now," he whines.

"You should do what your mom tells you," I say.

"See," his mother says. "Even Dellie thinks you should come in and eat."

She's cooking. Maybe she's learning.

"All right." Corey goes back into the apartment.

I think Miss Sandra has worked a miracle for Corey. I smile all the way up to my apartment.

"Mom, Corey's mother is cooking for him and she was nice to me."

"Really? That's great news, Dellie," my mother says. "I've been praying for this change."

Maybe it's my turn now.

Later on, I'm at my window when Kayla and Corey walk into the courtyard. I'm surprised to see them together, and a little jealous.

Corey's licking a vanilla ice-cream cone and it's dripping down his hand.

They sit on the bench and I guess Kayla can feel me staring because she looks up. I forget we're not friends anymore and almost wave. Kayla's hand lifts up from her lap for a second, then drops down to Corey's back. Did she forget too?

I hear Miss Shirley at the door. "Can I get you something to drink?" my mother says.

"No, no," Miss Shirley answers. "I don't mean to bother you, but I'm needin' a few *tings* from the Super Savings Mart and I was wondering if Dellie is available."

Anywhere but there, not even for Miss Shirley. The Super Savings Mart is across Bellmore Avenue, the street with Louis's makeshift shrine on the corner. I've only been back there once—for his memorial service—and I swore I'd never go anywhere near there again. "No, I can't. I'm busy," I say, coming into the room.

My father searches my face. "Doing what?"

"Cleaning my room."

My parents exchange glances. "You can do both," my mother says, taking my father's hand. "I trust you."

"I guess." I want to run back to my room, and lock the door.

"Glad to hear it, Dellie," Miss Shirley says, handing me money and her list.

By the time I get downstairs, Kayla and Corey are gone.

Bellmore Avenue is big and wide with stores up and down both sides. You can see it, and hear the traffic, way before you actually get to it.

When we were little, my mother used to take us to the shoe store there. The salesman gave us lollipops and rubbed Louis's head like he was making a wish, and afterward, we'd go to the pizzeria next door for lunch. Louis always got grape soda and I'd get root beer. Then we'd walk home, excited to show off our new shoes to my father or, if they were sneakers, we'd show him how fast they made us run. Louis made us laugh extra hard on the days he had that grape mustache.

I'm getting close, so I slow down. I'm barely moving. I could go back, say the store was closed, or maybe I should just go to another store, but then I remember Miss Shirley saying she can only get what she needs at the mart.

When I'm across the street from the store, I stop and watch a bunch of kids hanging out. I'm jealous of how they're all able to go about their business so easily.

Panic stirs in my chest and my heart starts beating double-time while I wait for the walk signal. I glance across the street just once to Louis's shrine. A few plastic flowers are still taped to the lamppost, but they've mostly lost their colors.

The light changes and I hurry to the other side and go straight into the store.

Inside, I load everything on the list into a handbasket and wait on the express line, which isn't exactly moving express-like.

I pay for the items and, just before leaving, I pause and take a deep breath. This time, I'll have to wait near the lamppost in order to get across the street.

It's starting to drizzle and the wind has picked up.

On the corner, waiting to cross, I try to ignore the shrine, but something bright catches my eye. I'd be able to get a better look in two steps, but I don't move.

The light changes and everyone crosses except me. It's raining harder now. Water is collecting in the gutter.

Instead of crossing at the next signal, I move closer to the lamppost and see that there's a fresh pink flower tucked in with the old ones.

Panic tries to grow, but I manage to fight it. Someone else has remembered Louis.

With another step, I'm almost directly in front of the lamppost. I search for a sign of who might've left it but find none.

Behind me, there's laughing but not belly laughing. It's smaller. Then, I hear Miss Shirley calling out to me at the exact same moment something tumbles off the curb. Without thinking, I step into the street. The grocery bag falls from my hand into the gutter. Miss Shirley's loaf of bread is now on the ground.

Wheels lock and slide across the wet street. A horn blows. My hand reaches out and I pull on a jacket with all my might. It's like I'm watching somebody else's hand, but when I feel the weight, I know it's mine.

We land in a puddle by the curb.

Supersister. I hear it in my heart and the panic is gone.

The car radio is playing and the driver has both hands on top of his head. He's yelling, "Oh my God!"

"Whoa, that was close," a voice says. I look over to find it's Corey I've saved. His eyes are wide and scared, but he's alive and it's because of me.

The driver kneels next to us. He's wearing a sweatshirt, a pair of dirty jeans and work boots. His breathing is loud and heavy like somebody was chasing him. "Don't move," he says, fumbling with his cell phone. "Come on, come on, work!"

A crowd is forming and someone asks what happened.

"That car was speeding and hit those two kids, I think," a woman says.

"No, it didn't. I was standing right here," a teenager adds. "That little boy ran into the street and that girl saved him. Neither one got hit."

Miss Shirley is carrying the biggest umbrella I've ever seen. "Why on earth were you going so fast?" she says to the driver.

"I'm so sorry!" The man's eyes tear up. "I didn't see them. It happened so quickly."

"Are you children all right?" Miss Shirley asks.

"Yes, I'm okay. Corey, are you hurt?" I point to his cast.

"I don't know, Dellie." He sits up carefully. "I don't think so."

"Don't move. It could be dangerous!" the man says, still trying to get his cell phone to work. "I'm trying to call for an ambulance."

"We're okay. We don't need an ambulance," I say, helping Corey to his feet. The crowd starts to break up. "You shouldn't be crossing the street by yourself. You're too little!" I say to Corey, feeling mad. "And why are you all the way over here alone? Where's your mother?"

"Home, I guess. Please don't be mad at me, Dellie. I didn't mean to run into the street. I was trying to run to you when I fell. That's all."

"It's just that if you got hurt," I blink back tears, "I'd be really sad."

"You would?"

"Of course!"

The man from the car starts to drive away, but not before Miss Shirley reminds him to drive more cautiously. He's going slowly, like he's afraid someone else might run into the street.

Miss Shirley holds her cane up a little. "Goodness," she says, looking toward the sky. "I've had enough rain for one day."

The rain slows to a drizzle and stops. "Are you a witch?" Corey asks.

Miss Shirley laughs. "No more than you are a billy goat."

On the way home, I thank Miss Shirley for calling my name when she did.

"But I didn't," she says.

"Yes you did, I heard it."

She shakes her head. "No, child. You're mistaken. The first words I spoke were to the driver of the car."

Her voice had been clear as it is right now. "Corey, didn't you hear Miss Shirley call me?"

"No, I didn't hear anything," he answers.

"What were you doing on Bellmore Avenue anyway, Miss Shirley?"

"I realized I needed some*ting* else," she says. "And I thought maybe I'd be able to catch up to you and let you know, but of course I'm not the world's fastest walker."

We're silent for the rest of the way, but my mind is racing. Thoughts of Louis's shrine try to make me sad, but I don't let them. It's now a place where a good thing has happened.

When we get to our building, I ask Miss Shirley if it'd be okay to go into her apartment to dry off before my parents see me.

"It's best you go and tell them what happened. I'll go with you if you'd like, but first let's get Corey home."

No one answers Corey's door, so he comes upstairs with us. He follows me to my door as Miss Shirley unlocks hers. "You think she's telling the truth about not being a witch, Dellie?" he whispers.

"Witches are only make-believe." But I'm not completely convinced anymore.

"Come on, little one," Miss Shirley says. "Let's get you dried off."

Corey tugs on my hand. "Can Dellie come too?"

"Okay, but only for a short while," Miss Shirley replies.

My mouth falls open when I see a vase full of fresh pink flowers sitting on Miss Shirley's table. "Did you put a flower on Louis's shrine by the Super Savings Mart?"

"What's a shrine?" Corey asks.

"Are you sure you're all right, Dellie? The only pink flowers I've seen today are the ones on my table," Miss Shirley answers.

First I'm hearing things and now I'm seeing things too. "You were standing right next to the lamppost. Are you sure you didn't see it? It was pink, just like these," I say, touching one of the flowers.

"It was raining and a little bit windy," Miss Shirley walks to her bedroom. "Maybe what you saw was a piece of paper that got blown there?"

Now, I'm not so sure . . .

"So, what's a shrine?" Corey asks impatiently.

"Well, Corey," Miss Shirley says, walking back in holding a towel, a shirt and a pair of socks, "it's a special place where you go to remember someone you love."

"Oh," he says. "Then that's a good place, right, Dellie?"

"Yes, it is," I say, looking into Miss Shirley's eyes.

"Can I come over in a little while?" Corey asks before I leave.

"Of course you can."

■   ■   ■

My parents are in the kitchen. I smile so they'll know I'm okay even though my clothes are wet and dirty from being in the puddle.

"Look at you," my mother says. "I know you were caught in the rain, but how did you get so dirty?"

"I fell in a puddle with Corey," I say.

"Did either of you get hurt?" my father asks.

"No . . . ," I say. "Corey almost did, but I guess I saved him."

"What happened, Dellie?" my mother asks. "How did he almost get hurt?" Her voice is sharp.

"Corey ran into the street on Bellmore Avenue." I say it fast. "But he wasn't hurt." I leave out the part about the flower and Louis's shrine.

My father watches my mother's reaction. "Then," she says, taking me in her arms, "it was a very good thing you were there."

I think about hearing my name and the flower. Maybe I was meant to be there.

My mother covers Corey in kisses when he comes over. "I'm so glad you're okay. Promise me you'll never go into the street again."

He closes his eyes and points his face upward for more kisses. "I promise, Miss Dellie's mama," he says, giggling. "I like kisses!"

When it's time for Corey to go home, I walk him to his apartment. The only noise I hear when he opens the door is the television.

I take my time going back up the steps. It's a mixed-up day for me. I'm happy about saving Corey, but sad I didn't save Louis. I should've been able to save him too.

Before I can open my door, I hear my name floating up from the first floor. It's Corey's mother calling me. At first, I'm nervous, but her voice isn't mean, so I'm not afraid.

"Corey told me what happened with the car. I was only out for a few minutes," she says when I reach her door. I'm surprised to see her looking so nice. She's wearing a skirt and I think she even has on some makeup. "I wanted to thank you. I don't know what . . ."—her voice cracks—"I would've done if something bad happened to him."

"You're welcome." She really does love him.

I go to bed early and I pray extra hard for Corey to always be safe. Then, I ask if it's all right for me to care for another little boy even though I hurt Louis. The minute I ask, I know it sounds crazy.

When I finally fall asleep, I dream of Louis again. We're playing hide-and-seek in a garden.

"I'm gonna find you!" I say.

There's movement behind a tree. When I get closer, I hear giggling. "Gotcha!"

"You found me! Here," he says and hands me a bouquet of pink flowers. "These are for you, Dellie."

When I wake up, there is a happiness inside me I can't describe.

TWENTY

I open my eyes two minutes before the alarm goes off. It's almost been a week since Bellmore Avenue and I'm still not sure if what I saw on the lamppost was a flower or a piece of paper like Miss Shirley said, but it's okay either way. Whatever it was put me right where I needed to be.

There's a note on the refrigerator door when I make my way to the kitchen.

> *Good morning, mami.*
> *You're on your own this morning . . .*

Wow! I get to walk to school without my father trailing behind me.

> *Just be careful, okay? We're going out to dinner after work tonight. We might go to a movie too. There's leftover chicken you can heat up or you can make yourself a sandwich. Have a good day at school.*

There's a heart drawn at the bottom of the note with *Mom and Dad* written in the middle of it.

Tonight is therapy night. I guess they're skipping it.

Alexa corners me outside math class. She's carrying a big yellow pad and a pen. "Mr. Dumbrewski wants us to set up our tutoring schedules." She gets ready to write something down. "What day is good for you?"

I wish Mr. Dumbrewski would just do the tutoring after school himself.

"For me? I don't need tutoring."

"Well, Mr. Dumbrewski said you do."

"He's wrong." I'm fuming. Teachers shouldn't be allowed to talk about who needs what to other people.

"Who's wrong?" It's Michael.

Now I'm burning with embarrassment. "Nothing."

Alexa takes a step closer to him. "Awww, Dellie, don't be embarrassed. We won't tell anybody how much help you need."

"I'm not." I give a little laugh like she's crazy. "Who said anything about being embarrassed?"

"Then why are you turning all red?"

The sight of Alexa standing there with her pad, trying to look official, is sickening. "Dumbrewski's wrong!" I start to walk away.

"Hellooo, no he's not," Alexa says. "He's the teacher. Don't you think he knows?"

I'm surprised when Kayla steps in for me. "Alexa, you're such a troublemaker." It isn't much, but at least it's something.

"I'm not talking to you," Alexa returns.

As we file into class, Michael slips me a note as Alexa walks by. "He doesn't like dumb girls, so give it up," she mumbles.

Nothing she says can upset me when I'm the one holding a note from Michael. Kayla watches me unfold it. *Alexa's a jerk. Can I walk you home later? I want to ask you something.*

This is big, bigger than big, even.

I write *Okay* on the note and slip it back to him just before the bell rings.

Mr. Dumbrewski sits on his desk, wearing a short-sleeved shirt. His arms are hairy.

The desks are arranged differently and we can't tell whose desk is whose, so we stand together tightly against the walls, waiting for an explanation.

When the last person walks in, Mr. Dumbrewski closes the door. "If you're awake, and you look like you are since your eyes are open, you may have noticed what I've done with your desks."

"I sleep with my eyes open all the time, especially when I'm at school," Xavier says.

Everyone giggles except me. I don't like surprises in math class.

Mr. Dumbrewski picks his pants up so that his belly is tucked into them a little more. "I can tell."

"Ooh, he dissed you," someone says under their breath.

"There are two people," Mr. Dumbrewski says, "in this class who, out of the goodness of their math-loving hearts, have volunteered to tutor those of you who lack any sort of math love." He deepens his voice on *love* like he's a radio DJ.

When Mr. Dumbrewski calls Alexa and Michael's names, Alexa pushes her way through.

Michael takes his time. He doesn't look happy about this at all.

"Not one of you has signed up," Mr. Dumbrewski says to the class. "So, I have taken the liberty of signing you *all* up." Some people grumble, me included. "I've divided you into two groups," Mr. Dumbrewski continues. "When I call your name, please sit at a desk to the right of the room."

My name is the last he calls before asking everyone else to sit to the left. When everyone has a seat, Mr. Dumbrewski explains that each group is like a team. Alexa and Michael are the captains.

I don't want to be on either team.

"Michael," Mr. Dumbrewski says, "please take a seat with the group on the right."

Alexa glares at me when Michael sits in the seat next to mine. "I wanted the right side, Mr. Dumbrewski!" she says in alarm.

"It really doesn't matter. Please take a seat with the group on the left," Mr. Dumbrewski answers.

I can't stop the laugh that comes half out of my nose. Michael nudges me with his shoulder in the tiniest way. "Oh, well," he says so only I'll hear. Now I really feel like we're a team.

Michael is a pretty good math captain and we're kind of having fun working on the problems Mr. Dumbrewski gives us. I never thought in a million years I'd ever think of math and fun at the same time.

"Michael," Mr. Dumbrewski says when we get too loud, "are you doing the math or are you taking the opportunity to play around?"

Alexa almost breaks her neck to see what we're doing. "I knew I should've been captain of that team," she says in a huff. "I would've whipped their butts right into shape, especially Dellie's."

"No, we're doing the work," Michael says, handing Mr. Dumbrewski the math sheet we've just finished.

Mr. Dumbrewski looks it over, then says, "Very good. Keep it up."

"Ha!" Xavier says, snapping his fingers in Alexa's face. "They don't need you. They're doing better than we are."

"Why do you always have something to say to me?" Alexa says.

"'Cause." Xavier shrugs. "You're annoying?"

They start arguing and Mr. Dumbrewski has to make them stop.

For the rest of the day, I go from excited to nervous a million times, thinking about what Michael has to ask me on the walk home. We've walked together before, but the note makes this time important.

When the last bell rings, I'm the first one out the door.

"Hey," Michael says in a serious tone when he sees me.

A breath gets caught in my throat. "Hey," I say back.

"You ready?" he asks.

"Yeah." I set our pace to slow so that the time we have together will last longer.

We walk in silence for a few minutes and it's killing me. I wish he'd just hurry up and ask me whatever it is. After another block, I can't take it anymore and start talking about the first thing that comes to mind. "The whole tutoring thing isn't as bad as I thought it was going to be." I pause, hoping he'll cut in, but he doesn't say a word. "'Cause me and math are like this," I say, spreading my arms out. "But somehow, you made it make sense."

"I can help you whenever you want," he finally says.

"Thanks."

"It's no big deal," he says at the corner. "I mean, I like you, so I don't mind."

"Really?" I'm smiling way too much.

"Yeah, and I was even wondering . . ."—he gets quiet again and I think I'm going to lose my mind—"if you wanted to be my girlfriend." His hair falls in front of his eyes, but he moves it out of the way. "You don't have to answer me right now. You can think about it if you want." Oh my God! My skin gets tingly. I don't need to think about anything.

When I nod, he takes my hand. "Cool." He smiles.

TWENTY-ONE

It's eight o'clock Sunday morning and I don't want to get up yet.

"Dellie," my mother calls sharply. Sleep leaves me for good at the sound of her voice.

Corey is sitting at the kitchen table in dirty pajamas when I come in. My father stands behind him.

Corey's cast is off and his injured arm looks smaller than the other. There's a big red scrape from his jaw down to his neck and it looks like he's been crying.

My stomach drops. His mother must've gone back to her old ways.

"Hey little man."

"Hi, Dellie," he answers, barely opening his mouth.

"Where's your mother?" I ask.

My mother is mixing up pancake batter. Pancakes were one of my brother's favorite foods. Sometimes my mother would let him eat them for dinner.

"I don't know. Her and Kendal left after I woke up," Corey says, showing us a key. "She said she's never coming back." A tear slips down his face.

"It's okay," I soothe. "You're with us now. Don't worry."

"But I want her . . . ."

The words won't come, so I just get on my knees and hug him while he cries. After a little while, he wipes his face. "Kendal took my cereal too. I tried to stop him but I couldn't. He was stronger. He pushed me down and that's how I got this," he says, pointing to the scrape. "I hit the side of the counter. Then he showed me a gun. Kendal's mean, Dellie."

I hope with everything inside me that somebody will push Kendal down. He's the one who deserves it, not Corey.

"A gun?" my mother says. Corey nods slowly.

I kiss Corey's cheek because I don't know what else to do. "Owww," he says, touching the scrape.

"I'm sorry!" My voice comes out shaky.

My father bends down to get a better look at it. Corey winces. "How could she let this happen?" he says to nobody.

"*Bebé pobre,*" my mother says, wiping her tears. Poor baby.

"Are you hurt anyplace else?" my father asks.

Corey gets nervous with all the attention. "No, but it's okay. It doesn't hurt too much."

We all watch Corey in silence like we're frozen. He puts

his head down on the table and spins the key around. "She said I wasn't worth so much work . . ."

"You're a sweet, smart boy," my mother says. "You're worth the world to us and I need you to always remember that."

Corey picks his head up and tears drop on the table. They're small and round. He shouldn't have to cry. "Am I like that boy in the picture?" he asks.

"Yes," my mother says, reaching for my father's hand. "You are."

Corey nods, then puts his head back on the table. "I'll remember."

"Are you hungry, baby?" my mother asks.

"Yes."

"How about some blueberry pancakes?" my mother says, rubbing Corey's back.

"I don't like to eat nothing blue," he says.

"Come on," I say. "You don't like *anything* blue?"

"What about blue lollipops or blue bubble gum, huh?" my father asks.

"That's different," he says, sitting up. "That's *candy*, not *food*."

My father makes a noise that sounds like the beginning of a laugh, but that's where it ends.

"Do you think if my mother makes you one tiny, baby blueberry pancake, you would at least try it?" I ask.

"Uhhh, if it's a real baby one," he says, holding his thumb and pointer finger together. "I'll try it. Can I put lots of syrup on it?"

"Of course, Corey. You can have as much syrup as you want," my father answers.

In the kitchen, I ask my mother if I should call Miss Sandra. She nods without saying a word.

I use the phone in my parents' bedroom. I dial Miss Sandra's home number and a woman answers on the fourth ring.

"Hello, can I speak to Miss Sandra, please?"

The voice on the other end sounds sleepy. "Yes, this is Miss Sandra Cumberland."

"Oh, hi, Miss Sandra. This is Dellie."

"Dellie . . . ?"

"You know, Corey's friend."

"Oh, yes, Dellie!" she says. "How are you?"

"Well, I'm okay, but"—I take a deep breath—"Corey's mother left him."

"What do you mean?"

"He told us his mother said he was too much work, so she left when Corey woke up this morning." I swallow, trying to keep calm. Then I think about Kendal, and my voice gets loud and uneven. "And her boyfriend pushed him down. He has a scrape on his neck."

I don't think I'll ever be able to stop hating Kendal or wondering how Corey's mother could give up so fast. "Do you think she'll ever come back?" I ask.

"It's hard to say. Where is Corey now?" she asks.

"He's sitting with my parents. My mother's making him breakfast."

"Okay, Dellie. Can he stay with you until I can get there?"

"Of course, Miss Sandra. I . . . love him . . ."

"Oh, sweetie, I know you do. I'll be there in an hour. You live on the second floor, right?"

"Yes, Miss Sandra. Apartment 2E."

Quietly I tell my mother what Miss Sandra said.

"I guess if anyone would know about these things, it would be her," Mom says, shaking her head.

After Corey is done eating his third blueberry pancake, which swam in butter and syrup, my father cleans Corey up with a washcloth, slowly, so he doesn't hurt him.

"Thank you. You're nice," Corey says in a whisper. His eyes are closed.

My father softly clears his throat. "So are you."

TWENTY-TWO

While we wait for Miss Sandra, my father reads Corey the Sunday comics.

"Dellie, we need some clothes and underwear for Corey," my mother says as she fills the tub up for him.

"Can't he wear . . ."

"Wear what?"

I'm afraid to answer, but then she smiles.

"Louis's clothes?"

My mother pours the bubble bath into the running water. "They won't fit," she says.

"Something might. We should at least try."

Her eyes look thoughtful, like she's remembering. "Louis was much bigger than Corey is." She's right. He loved to eat. "I'll get Louis's Spider-Man towel," she says. "You think Corey likes Spider-Man?"

"All little boys like Spider-Man . . ."

"I guess you're right." She pours extra bubble bath into the water. "Do you think you could go down to Corey's apartment to see if you can find something for him to wear?"

I nod.

Even though his mother isn't home, I'm nervous. When I'm almost to the first floor, I stand still and listen. There's no noise at all except for the hum of the elevator. Corey's door is open just a little. I stand in the doorway and listen some more. The bullet hole stares back at me, reminding me this apartment is a dangerous place for Corey. I step inside.

In the bedroom, an open bag sits on the floor next to the mattress. I'm glad to see that it's filled with Corey's clothes. I don't want to take the time to look through the whole bag, so I grab it, slinging it over my shoulder. Suddenly, something falls somewhere in the apartment and I'm not sure which way to run.

I slowly step out of the bedroom, and stop in my tracks when I see Kayla standing in the doorway. She's carrying a plastic bag filled with cookies.

"I dropped this juice box when I took it out of my pocket," she says, holding it up. "It's Corey's favorite."

I don't say anything. I just stare at her.

"What're you doing in here anyway?" Kayla finally asks. "And where's Corey?" Kayla doesn't wait for an answer. She walks around the apartment. "Well, where is he?"

I continue to stare.

"Dellie, I have to tell you something." She sounds like the old Kayla. "I know it wasn't you," she says. "It was Sophia. Her uncle works in the building I used to live in and he knew all about my mother selling our stuff."

Even though I'm happy she finally believes me, I'm still mad. "Whatever," I say, moving past her.

Kayla doesn't have a choice but to move out of my way. "God, Dellie! I'm trying to tell you I'm sorry!" she yells after me. But I don't want to hear her sorry.

Corey is still in the tub when I return. He comes out wrapped in Louis's towel. My dad gives him an apple and they both sit on the couch and watch television.

My mother pulls a pair of Corey's superhero underwear, a pair of jeans, a faded T-shirt and a pair of stained socks out of the bag.

"Hey little man, come here," I call.

He walks over smelling like bubbles and soap. "I found your stuff, so get dressed, okay?"

But he doesn't answer me. "What is it? Is something hurting you?" I ask, thinking about the scrape.

"Why did she leave, Dellie? Am I bad?"

I kneel down so that we're face-to-face. "No, Corey, you aren't bad at all. You're the nicest kid I know." I put my hand on his damp head. "Everything will be okay. I called Miss Sandra. She'll know what to do."

"My mother's gonna be *mad*," he says in a low voice.

"Why will she be mad?"

"'Cause she hates Miss Sandra. She says Miss Sandra thinks she's better than her. She said she wants to beat the poop out of her."

"The poop?" I laugh.

"Well, you know. She used that other word." Corey puts his hand up to the side of his mouth and whispers, "The *s*-word."

We're both laughing when somebody knocks on the apartment door.

"That's probably Miss Sandra," I say, hugging him. "Time to get dressed."

Miss Sandra is carrying a briefcase but wearing a pair of jeans, sneakers and a sweatshirt. She looks nothing like when I first met her.

She shakes both my parents hands.

When everyone's introduced themselves, I pull out a chair for Miss Sandra. I sit down too, feeling tired.

"Dellie, thank you for calling me."

"I didn't know what else to do."

"Can I get you something to drink, Miss Cumberland?" my father asks.

"No, thank you, and please, call me Sandra."

My mother takes her apron off and sits next to me. My father sits at the head of the table like always.

"You did the right thing, Dellie. Where is Corey now?" Miss Sandra asks.

"He's in the bathroom getting dressed."

Miss Sandra removes a folder full of papers from her briefcase. "I'll have to take Corey to a foster family until I can find a relative who can care for him," she says, flipping through some forms.

Thinking about Corey leaving here to live with strangers triggers my panic. My hands begin to shake and I start to sweat. I never would've wanted my brother to live with people he didn't know.

"Will he be safe in a foster home, Miss Sandra? I mean, with strangers?"

"Dellie," my mother says, calming me down, "if it wasn't safe, I'm sure Miss Sandra wouldn't even suggest it."

"Your mother is right," Miss Sandra says, placing the papers on the table. "You don't have to worry. He'll be safe. I'll see if the foster family who cared for him before will be able to take him back for a bit. They have a son, Jayden, who is Corey's age and they had a lot of fun together."

"He went to a foster home before?" I ask.

"Yes." She leans back in her chair. "It's not a bad thing, Dellie. Sometimes people need to take a time-out and learn how to deal with things in a new way. His mother needed to do just that and Corey needed to be placed in a safe and loving environment for a short period of time."

"If you don't mind me asking," my mother says, "why was he returned to his mother so fast?"

"She attended a strict parenting program and showed progress quickly. Sometimes a parent needs to be taught what comes naturally to others."

"No offense, of course, to you, Sandra, but I think the program needs some adjusting." My mother shakes her head.

"Believe me, I understand where you're coming from. It's just how the system works."

"But are you sure he'll be okay, because you know, he could stay here with us. Right, Mom?"

If he stayed here, he could have Louis's room and Louis's toys.

"Oh, Dellie," Miss Sandra says before my mother can answer. "That's very sweet, but it's just not possible. There's a long process to clear foster homes for children and Corey needs a home right now, today. He can't wait for your family to be cleared."

My father leans forward. "He'll be fine with Jayden and his family. Try not to worry, mami."

"Do you think you can call us to let us know that he's all right, that he's being taken care of?" my mother asks.

"Yeah, because"—my voice breaks—"I'll still be worried about him."

"Of course I'll call you, Dellie." To my mother she says, "I want you to know I think Dellie is very special."

"Thank you. We couldn't have asked for a better daughter." My mother takes my hand.

I have a hard time swallowing the lump in my throat.

The bathroom door opens and Corey comes flying out. "Miss Sandra!" He runs to her and hugs her.

"Hi, honey," Miss Sandra says.

"I want my mama back," Corey cries.

"I know you do, but for now, would you like to visit Jayden and his mommy and daddy again?"

"Can't I stay here, Miss Sandra? Dellie's mama makes really good blue pancakes and her daddy reads real good. Pleeeease?"

My mother goes back into the kitchen. I feel her sadness. It feels the same as mine.

"No, honey. I'm sorry. You can't stay here, but you'll see Dellie and her mama and daddy again, okay?"

Corey runs behind me and holds on to my clothes. His grip is strong.

"No, Miss Sandra! It's nice here. And they like me, right, Dellie? Right? You and your mama and daddy like me? I don't even bother them like I bothered my mama. I'll be good and quiet, Miss Sandra, I promise!"

I reach behind me so that I can get a hold on him. "Yes, Corey, we really, really like you. . . . I . . ."

Corey stamps his feet. "So don't make me go . . . please!"

"You can come and visit me, I swear."

My father moves to our side of the table. "I'll read the comics to you when you visit. You liked them, didn't you? You sure were giggling a lot."

I feel Corey shaking his head against my back.

My mother comes out of the kitchen carrying the pajamas Corey was wearing when he came to us this morning. They're washed and folded. She is also carrying a plastic container filled with the extra blueberry pancakes. Without saying a word she puts everything on the table. Her eyes are red and her nose is running.

"Baby, you'll be okay at Jayden's house. They like you too," she says, kneeling in front of him. "And I know you'll make them happy, just like you've made us."

Corey's voice is quiet. "No . . ."

Miss Sandra pries his hands off me. "You'll see Dellie again, sweetie. Don't worry," she says in a soft voice.

My mother opens her arms and Corey falls into them. They stay that way for a long time.

"It's all right, baby," my mother says. "We'll see you again. It's okay to go now because it won't be forever. I promise. And you can share your blue pancakes with Jayden."

"What if he thinks blue food is weird?" Corey asks.

"Well, maybe you can show him just how good blue food can be," my mother says.

"Maybe."

Before Corey leaves, my mother gives him Connie Boy. "Take this with you, and whenever you feel sad," she says, "hug him up tight and think of us."

"Are you ready, Corey?" Miss Sandra asks.

He clutches Connie Boy and they're gone.

TWENTY-THREE

Even though my teachers handed out lots of work to get done over summer vacation, I'm glad it's finally here.

Mr. Dumbrewski will be our official math teacher next year. He's much better than Mrs. Robertson ever was. I got a C plus on my report card, thanks to Michael tutoring me.

Michael invited me to go to the mall with him and his friends after lunch. My parents said I can go, but first I have to go to the store to buy hamburger meat for dinner tonight. My mother is making tacos just because I asked for them.

"Don't forget the sour cream and tomatoes," she calls over the radio.

Miss Shirley's door is open. Her music is playing again and I smell banana bread. She's mopping her floors, wearing a deep purple dress that comes down to her ankles. Her braids hang over her shoulders. Gray hair is weaved into them.

"Where is it you are going to so early?" she says when I knock.

"Hi, Miss Shirley. I'm going to the store for my mother. Do you need anything?"

Before she can answer, Kayla comes down the steps. She's holding a cigarette between her fingers and she's singing. She stops when she sees me and Miss Shirley.

"What's up, Dellie?" The cigarette dances nervously from finger to finger.

Miss Shirley watches Kayla with lowered eyelids, almost like she's about to go to sleep. "Humph." She pushes it out like she has a bad taste in her mouth.

"Nothing," I answer Kayla.

"Yes, Dellie. I do need some items from the store. I have a list written out already. It was like I knew you'd ask!" Miss Shirley opens her door wider. "Come on in. I'll get it for you. You too, Kayla girl."

Kayla's eyes widen. "Me?" she asks.

"Yes, you," Miss Shirley says. "Don't you know those cigarettes will surely eat up your lungs like ants on sugar, young lady?"

"It's not mine." She tucks the cigarette into her hand. Still, the tip peeks out.

"Now why don't you come in for a nice warm slice of bread? I just took it out of the oven."

"It's banana bread," I say before Kayla thinks it's the boring white kind.

Kayla stares into Miss Shirley's apartment. From the doorway, you can see the half-moon painting. I wonder what she thinks of it.

"Are you coming in, Kayla?" Miss Shirley asks.

Kayla scans the room. Her curiosity gets the best of her. "Okay." She picks up a photo and holds it close to her face. It's a picture of a boy wearing a suit. "Who's this?" she asks.

"That is my brother, and those"—Miss Shirley sweeps her hand toward the other pictures—"are the rest of my people."

"They're dressed pretty normal," Kayla says, wrinkling up her nose. "So, how come you dress kind of . . . crazy?"

"Miss Shirley isn't crazy," I say.

"No," Kayla says. "I didn't mean it like that."

"I dress like this because it's different and I like it," Miss Shirley says. "I'm not one to worry about what others think of me or how fast their tongues wag, you know? I stay true to myself and always have." She pauses. "That's some*ting* you need to learn, Kayla girl."

Kayla nods. "I'm sorry," she says.

She seems to always think those two words will make everything better.

"Apology accepted," Miss Shirley says. I think she let Kayla off the hook too easily.

I sit on the opposite end of the couch from where Kayla watches silently.

Miss Shirley sits between us. A grunt puffs out of her, not from her mouth but from somewhere in her throat.

She smells powdery like she just got out of the bath.

We sit for a little while listening to the music. I'm so comfortable here. If I closed my eyes, I'd fall right to sleep.

"I miss Corey, you know?" It slips out of me before I can stop it. "A week without seeing him is too long."

Miss Shirley squeezes my hand. "Yes. Yes, I do know. I believe in here," she says, holding her other hand to her chest, "that Corey will be just fine."

"Where did Corey go, exactly?" Kayla asks.

"To live with a foster family somewhere. Why?"

"Because I care about what happens to him," Kayla answers. "I care about a lot of things."

"You didn't care when Bryan made it look like I was stealing or when the kids at school teased me for it," I spit out.

"Dellie," Miss Shirley says. "Calm down."

"It's okay, Miss Shirley," Kayla says. "She's right. I should've done something both times." She starts picking her nail polish off. "Was Corey okay when he left?"

I don't answer.

Kayla sits forward to get a better look at me. "Come on, Dellie. I did things for him too."

"Please, not as much as I did, sneaking him food."

"I did as much as I could without my mother knowing," Kayla says. Kayla's tears run down her face faster than she can wipe them. I'm sorry for ever starting this, but I don't know how to stop it.

"Yeah, well—"

"Dellie, you're not the only one with problems," Kayla says, cutting me off. "I might not have a brother who got killed, but I know what it's like to . . ."

Panic shuts everything down and I can't hear the rest of what Kayla says. I take a deep breath like I've been underwater too long, and bolt for the door. But Miss Shirley takes hold of me. I can't see her. Everything is just a bunch of colors running together.

I don't fight her. I cover my face with both hands and let the tears come.

"It is good to get *tings* out," Miss Shirley says.

"Dellie, I'm sorry. I'm sorry for everything." Kayla's voice is low and unsure. She carefully pulls one hand away from my face, then the other, and when she looks into my eyes, I know she means it. "Please don't be mad at me anymore, okay? I'll even go back to the store with you to tell them it was Bryan who put all that stuff into your pocket," she says. I think I finally have my friend back.

The half-moon on the wall reminds me of what Miss Shirley said about faith being powerful. How it'll help you to believe something even when you can't see it. I close my eyes, praying and hoping with my whole self for Miss Shirley's faith. I want it to rush me to the other side of my grief.

"Trouble no set like rain," Miss Shirley says.

"What does that mean?" Kayla asks.

"It's a saying from Jamaica. It means we're rarely warned of bad times approaching, the way storm clouds might warn of bad weather. You had no idea of the dark cloud awaiting you and your brother that day, Dellie. You are not to blame."

Those last few words echo inside me.

"I know what it's like to lose someone so close and to feel the blame of it," Miss Shirley says.

I wonder if she's talking about her sister Aggie.

"I'll make us some peppermint tea," Miss Shirley says, shaking her head. "We need to send these bad feelings on their way for good."

We sit at Miss Shirley's kitchen table while she makes the tea. My eyelids are fat from crying.

I catch a glimpse of Kayla's cigarette. "So if that's not yours, whose is it?"

"Bryan's. He thinks smoking is cool, so I let him think I did too. I was going to throw it out so my mother wouldn't find it."

Kayla opens her hand. The cigarette is flattened. Pieces of tobacco are stuck to her sweaty palm.

"I did see you smoking," I say.

"I only did it that once and it was terrible. I thought my throat was on fire."

Miss Shirley brings our tea over to us. "I'm out of lemon, but it's on the list." She takes a piece of paper from her pocket along with the ten-dollar bill and hands them to me.

"Miss Shirley?" I ask before I lose my nerve. "What happened to your sister?"

"Not too long after that picture was taken of us," she says, pointing to the table, "there was a fire in my house." Miss Shirley stops to take a sip of tea, but I know she's really stopping to line up her words in order to push them out. "My parents were working late like they sometimes did. So I fixed supper. A little while later, we went to sleep. When the smell woke me up, I knew there was fire burning somewhere close. The smoke was thick and burned at my eyes as I ran into Aggie's room. When I reached her bed, I felt around for her, but she wasn't there."

My heart is thumping in my ears. I take a drink of my tea. Kayla hasn't even touched her cup. Her eyes are glued to Miss Shirley.

"I could not yell her name so hard because every time I tried, the smoke was sucked down my throat. There were flames everywhere. I had no choice but to jump out of the window."

Kayla puts her hand over her mouth. I guess Miss Shirley's jumping out the window is the reason why she limps the way she does.

"Everyone in my little village came to help with buckets of water, even the really old people," Miss Shirley continues. "I thought maybe I'd forgotten that Aggie was sleeping at a friend's house and that was why I couldn't find her in her bed, but then I remembered the real reason I could not find her. She was sleeping in the extra bedroom that night because it was cooler in there. It faced the ocean and the breeze was beautiful. So you see, there was no warning of dark clouds for me either."

I want her to stop talking. I know what happened. I don't need her to say the words.

"I tried to go back into the house, but the neighbors would not let me. I fought and fought until I could not move anymore. It wasn't until later that I realized I had been hurt. And"—Miss Shirley sighs long and sad—"I never saw my Aggie again."

"That's terrible," Kayla says.

"I'm sorry about your sister," I say.

"And I'm sorry about your brother," Miss Shirley answers.

"Louis." I say his name once, then again, "Louis was his name."

"I'm sorry about Louis," Miss Shirley says.

There is an awkward silence before Miss Shirley breaks it. "So every*ting* between you two cook and curry?"

"Huh?" we answer.

"It means all is well, all is taken care of."

Kayla takes my hand and we both nod.

"Yup, all cooked and curried and stuff," Kayla answers.

"Yes," Miss Shirley adds. "I believe it is, all of it, one hundred percent."

I look at the half-moon. Only it doesn't seem like it's missing a piece of itself. It's there now. It's been there all along.

ACKNOWLEDGMENTS

Thank you to my incredibly sharp editor, Stacey Barney, for helping me to sculpt my story into a book.

I'd also like to thank my agent, Caryn Wiseman, for encouraging me early on when I thought the road had ended. You never know how far your words will take a person.

Thank you to the kind and generous people who hang out at the Blueboard.

A big thank-you to my husband, Sal, for listening to me, for brainstorming with me and for being the best husband anyone could ever ask for. And most importantly, for never complaining about the tall piles of laundry lurking in the basement.

To my girls, Mia and Ami. You bring me great joy every day.

And to my extended family for all of your support along the way, and especially to Michele for reading and believing in me even when I didn't.

And of course, thanks to the Big Guy Upstairs.